Knowing Josie Martin

Susan Higgins

Contents

Prologue

I stare into cold, unforgiving eyes. The blade clasped in her pale, bony hand. Her sharp, claw-like painted black nails a striking contrast against her ivory complexion.

I regret coming here now. I should have stayed away but, in true 'Martin' form, I cannot just accept things for how they are. I've spent my whole life with my eyes forced closed and now they have opened, I have no way of shutting them again. Knowing what I know has led me straight into the Lion's Den and the Lioness is in front of me, waiting to pounce.

Inhaling a shaky breath and balling my hands into fists, I take another step towards her. Her mouth twisting up in the most feral, sinister smile. The blade in her hand glinting against the dim light.

There is no escape.

To every single one of my friends, you have no idea how much I love each of you. Thank you for supporting me and always making the time to listen to my crazy ideas. You're all so amazing and I'm blessed to have you in my life. All my love always.
Thank you to my old English Teacher for pushing me to persue literature.

Chapter 1, Josie:

I've been sat in this white room for far too long now and I just want to go home... home. Where is that exactly?

Nick's home cannot be mine anymore, not after what I have been put through. It would only be a matter of time before I am fed more lies and finding out more secrets I would rather not uncover.

Nick is the reason I am here. If he had told me sooner, then I may have been able to find it in me to hear him out. Sadly, that is not the route he chose to take. Instead he told both mine and his best friends first. His Uncle knew, along with my Mum... Who should be dead? I'm still left wondering if my Stepmother and Dad know the truth or not?

It will make sense if they do, it will explain my Stepmother's hate for me. But then again, if my Stepmother knew, she would be spiteful enough to dangle it in my face. Wouldn't she?

The pulsating pain in my side brings me back to the real world. A Nurse enters the room holding a clipboard. His spare hand drags along an observation machine equipped with a blood pressure cuff, an ear temperature taker thing, and a pulse recorder that will be put on the end of my finger. Since arriving at hospital, I must have had my observations recorded at least thirty times already.

That is an exaggeration, but it feels like it. The worst of them all is the blood pressure cuff, I'm sure it will end up getting so tight that my arm will drop off.

The thought makes me feel queasy and I chuckle to myself. My nurse is so lovely. He is newly qualified and went into nursing when his own Daughter ended up unwell. The care his Daughter received was so exemplary that he felt the need to give back. He told me his name is Matthew. Matthew has a smile that distracts from the clinical environment that surrounds us.

My blood pressure is checked, along with my temperature and pulse. Matthew explains my blood pressure is still a bit high as a result of my concussion, but my heart rate and temperature do not seem to be a concern, Matthew assures me.

Matthew explains that they would like to keep me in overnight just for observation, so I will be moved up to a ward within the hour.

I am now left on my own in the emergency room. Nick was made to sit in the waiting area whilst I was seen to and I worry that he is still there now. I cannot face him... I've kept it together pretty well, but one push and I will crumble.

A loud bang causes me to snap my head to the left a bit too fast and stars appear across my vision. I quickly blink them away and take some deep breaths, pushing through the pain my broken ribs are causing me.

The bang comes from a drunk who is staggering around his little cubicle. He is incoherent, shouting abuse at the poor Porter who is stood a safe distance away. The Porter looks terrified and, if I were stable enough, I feel that I would be over there defending the poor lad. Before I have time to think about doing such a thing, I spot a flash of black in my peripheral vision. Nick...

He is making his way towards me, accompanied by my Nurse Matthew.

Nick stops dead in his tracks and glares at the disruptive drunk.

Uh-oh. Instinctively I know what Nick is thinking.

In a heartbeat, Nick is in the cubicle housing the drunk. Nick pins him to the bed.

"There are more important problems going on around you right now. People with more severe problems that need help. Maybe you should take that into consideration before you neck your next bottle, eh? Now, apologise." Nick points to the Porter who now stands tall and proud. I notice him wink at Nick and the drunk fixes his gaze to the porter.

"Sorry... I guess." Nick loosens his grip on the guy.

"Good, now stay silent and wait to be seen." With that, Nick finally looks at me. He saunters towards me and I cannot do anything but look around the room, trying not to meet his eyes.

I smile at Matthew, silently begging him to come and speak to me so that I can avoid Nick for a few moments longer.

My silent prayers are answered, and Matthew appears at my side.

"How are you doing? Are you in any pain? Shouldn't be much longer now before you are taken up." I am in pain. Each breath is like being stabbed over and over. I have possibly the worst headache I have ever experienced.

"My ribs hurt, and I do have a headache. What exactly are you keeping an eye out for overnight?" My last question to Matthew feels irrelevant but Nick has now joined us, and I would rather not speak to him for as long as I can manage.

"Okay love, we're just monitoring to ensure you are not sick, that you do not pass out or that nothing happens that make indicate a Subdural Hematoma," My cocked head tells Matthew that the medical term means nothing to me.

"Sorry, basically because you have a head injury, we need to make sure it is not anything serious like bleeding on the brain." I gulp. I feel okay right now. I have not felt anything else besides this headache and rib pain.

"Well let us just hope for the best! I'm okay at the moment, I hope nothing serious happens." I smile at Matthew, hoping to take away some of the seriousness from the situation. Nick responds by placing his hand on my shoulder in a supportive manner.

I do my best to shrug off his hand without causing myself more pain. Nick does not budge which only further fuels my anger towards him.

I glance sideways at Nick, silently cursing him. Nick's eyes are boring into Matthew and whatever he appears to be doing works. Matthew bows his head at me and then leaves.

~

Nick's eyes burn into mine as he comes to stand in front of me. I expect him to tilt my head up, forcing me to look at him. I am surprised when he doesn't do so. I suddenly realise that he isn't sure whether he can touch me, more than likely worried that he will hurt me. If only that were his train of thought when it comes to my feelings.

"Josie... I don't even know where to start. Are you okay? Are we okay?" He really has some nerve. He knows I am far from okay, both physically and emotionally. As for us... My brain cannot think about that right now. I was sure Nick was my hero, but now I'm not so sure. I just feel like everyone is out to hurt me. Right now, I need space from everyone to figure things out. The only problem with that is the looming question of 'where do I go?'

When Sarah was delivering her warning to me, she assured me I would always have her to rely on, that I was not without options should I find myself unable to live with Nick. Sarah was a part of all of this though. I know that Sam told her the day we met in the coffee shop and Sam had phoned her. As soon as Sarah had come back to the table following that phone call, she had been different. Little did I know back then that my Best Friend was also keeping the truth from me.

Chapter 2, Nick:

I really do not know what I expected. Did I really expect to reveal a colossal secret like that to her and for her to just accept it with open arms? As if. It would have been wonderful if that is the way it went, but sadly that was not the case. I should have told her when it was just the both of us, alone. I should not have told my Uncle of my plans. If I had kept it between myself and Josie, then I could have just been a shoulder for her. I would have sat on the floor of the Study with her, my arms holding her tight. I would have held her safe and I would have explained everything that happened, from my Uncle's admission, to my own discovery.

It is always easy to say 'I would have' when it is too late, and the damage has been done.

~

The car had struck her, and my world had collapsed. Josie lay in a heap on the gritty road. The driver had flown from the car to Josie's side, apologising profusely. The driver, a man in his late Forties with large, black framed glasses and slicked back hair was shell-shocked. He kept repeating how Josie had 'come out of no-where.' As unlike me as it was, I had pulled the bloke into a hug. It was not his fault at all, a case of wrong place wrong time. A woman around the same age as the man sat in the passenger seat, stunned. She had visibly collected herself and had rushed from the car to come to Josie's aid, her phone pressed to her ear as she phoned for an ambulance. I learnt that the bloke's name is Philip and his wife is Beth. The pair were travelling to their Son's wedding reception before colliding with Josie. The Police had arrived just before the ambulance. A breathalyser test was performed on

Philip, of course coming back clear. I had mumbled numerous apologies over this. Philip looked so embarrassed through the whole ordeal, all the while my subconscious screamed at me that I'm at fault for this incident even occurring.

The ambulance had arrived, and Josie was placed on a stretcher. I rode with her to the hospital, sitting away from her as the paramedics checked her over. I just wanted to go to her, to hug her and apologise over and over. When she had woken, her piercing blue eyes had met mine, betrayal etched all over her perfect, pale face.

~

I'm now sat across from Josie in this small, suffocating emergency room as we wait for her to be taken to a ward. I wish she could come home with me tonight. I need her with me. I'm being selfish, one of the only reasons I want her with me is because I fear when I return tomorrow, she will have already left. It isn't like I don't deserve it…

Josie still has not answered my question. I need to know if she is okay if WE are okay. She looks ahead, her breathing shallow but controlled. She blinks rapidly and it takes every ounce of my will power not to place myself in front of her, so she is forced to look at me. I think better of this though, knowing it will only add fuel to an already ablaze fire.

After I feel like I have held my breath for long enough, I exhale just as Josie begins to speak.

"Nick, I am so tired. Like, beyond any sort of tired you could comprehend. You do not want to know my thoughts right now. Please just leave, give me space. We can talk tomorrow." Josie still looks blankly ahead. Her voice monotone, as if she has no emotion left to give.

"Are you sure that is what you want? If you would like me to leave, then I will. If you need me, I will come straight back, okay?" Josie noticeably swallows the lump in her throat. I know she is hurting and against my better judgement, I know she needs space.

Space from me. Space from the whole fucked up situation. The love I have for this girl goes beyond my selfishness.

"Yes, Nick. Please just go. I'll call you if I need you, but I know I won't. I needed you to tell me the truth, but you didn't." The words slice through me like a hot butter knife. I had given Josie her phone as soon as we got to the hospital. Without her knowing, I had deleted the message Martha sent. Josie does not need that shit right now. I will deal with the wrath later.

I stand and give her the most gently hug. I want to kiss her; tell her I love her. She remains statue like, not reciprocating my hug in any way. I feel broken but I knew that I would. I pull away and give her the smallest smile I can manage, telling her goodbye silently.

~

I arrive back home just as it gets dark. The house feels empty... My Uncle's Jeep sits grandly in the drive, so I know he is here. I go to flick the hallway light on, the bulb flickers before blowing. This is all I fucking need!

I squeeze my eyes shut and draw as much air into my lungs as they can accept. With all my energy I begin to scream. It's the most feral scream that has ever escaped my body. Come to think of it, I do not think I have ever screamed once in my life. The sound coming out of me could shatter the windows. I keep going until all that is left is a mere squeak. I repeat the process of drawing air and opening my mouth to scream again. A silhouette in the shape of my Uncle appears at the top of the stairs. Racing towards me, he leans forward to put his hands on my shoulders. I manage to evade his grip. I must look crazy, staring straight into my Uncle's glowing eyes as I screech with tears cascading down my inflamed face. My Uncle surprises me by pulling me into a bear hug. I try to wriggle free. I never knew my Uncle had such strength. I flail around in my Uncle's arms, beating my fists pathetically into his chest. My Uncle makes little 'oomph' noises as my fists connect with his tough chest muscles.

"It's okay Lad, let it all out." I want to tell him to shut up. To leave me alone. I just cannot find the words to say so. My energy is dissolving so I finally rest against my Uncle. Fuck this... I wrap my arms around the middle section of my Uncle's body, giving into the hug he unwillingly pulled me into.

~

"There we go Lad; a cup of cocoa always makes things a little bit better." I bring the steaming mug up to my lips, welcoming both the scent and the warm steam as it hits my face. My Mum would always make a hot chocolate for both of us after my Dad had done something stupid and walked out for the night. As I am reminiscing, I feel my Uncle watching me intently.

"What?" I make no attempt to mask my rude tone as I snap at my Uncle.

"I am just so proud of the young person you have turned in to. Josie makes you a better man." Bile rises in my throat. Under any other circumstance, I would have been overjoyed at these words.

"Why me? Why did you tell me? You could have just kept the whole thing hidden from me. Yes, I would have been pissed but at least Josie would be here and not in a hospital." My Uncle looks down into his mug, guilt evident as he taps his fingers on the rim.

"When I first showed up and saw her, I knew she was Martha's Daughter instantly. Martha had shown me pictures. I did not want to be deceitful with you. I felt that lying to you would be so much worse than telling you the truth. I thought that by telling you, you could break the news gently to Josie." I am aware of the scowl I am giving my Uncle and if looks could kill, my Uncle would be on the kitchen floor rather than sitting here. I am about to respond when my Uncle raises a hand, halting the harsh words that would have tumbled from my mouth.

"There is so much more to tell you, but I think Martha owes it to Josie to tell her personally. I've already said enough." He thinks?! Hell, he should not have ever uttered a word to me in the first place!

"Okay. Well it has been a long day, to say the least. I'm going to get off to bed. Thanks for the drink." I raise my mug at my Uncle in a toasting fashion.

Thanks to the lack of light in the hall, I just about find my way to the stairs without stumbling. My Uncle follows suit, apparently planning to turn in for the night also. Without thinking, I stop by Josie's room. Everything is as she left it. The bedsheets still over-turned and college books littering one of the tables beside the bed. Before I realise it, I am halfway into the room.

"She's the best thing that has ever happened to you, Lad. She will come around. Just be there for her." Before I can respond, my Uncle pulls the door closed and I am left standing in Josie's room praying that my Uncle is right in what he says. She's my world, the light in the darkness and definitely the best thing that ever happened to me. I set the cup of warm cocoa onto the empty be-side table and flick on the lamp. I climb in amongst the mound of duvet and blankets, snuggling down and drinking in the scent of Josie. I know she more than likely will not respond, but I cannot help sending her a quick text to let her know I am thinking of her and that I love her.

Sleep is overcoming me, and I fight it as best as I can. It's coming on to midnight and I know I am absolutely shattered from the emotional turmoil that the past day has dealt out. I shut my eyes and pray for a peaceful sleep.

Chapter 3, Josie:

The ward is peaceful. Yes, I am surrounded by other people, but they have all been friendly so far. The nurses keep checking on me, but it does not irritate me in the slightest. I'm not judged here, no one knows my circumstances. They only know that I was hit by a car. Anything could have happened leading up to that. I could have just stumbled into the road accidentally, a clumsy mistake on my part. I wish that were the truth.

I've pushed the thought of having to go home tomorrow to the back of my mind. An irrational thought crosses my mind, 'what if I tell them I'm feeling worse, will I be able to stay another night?' I know this is not fair though. Someone else will need this bed more than me, I'm being selfish.

My phone buzzes beside me and I glance to see a message from Nick. The irresponsible side of me thinks to respond but I decide against it, deleting the message and switching my phone off, tucking it away under my pillow.

I survey the ward, questioning the reasons behind the other patient's stay here. There is a girl across from me, roughly the same age. After speaking to her briefly earlier on, I learnt that her name is Katie and she's here due to a broken ankle.

"Playing football is a dangerous sport," she had laughed to me. When asking why I am here, I simply replied with "I'm just clumsy, I should have looked before crossing the road," Katie had looked at me in questioning, but she didn't press the matter. Katie doesn't strike me as being dim-witted, but she is not one to pry, I appreciate that.

My body is begging me for sleep, but I just cannot shut off. I still have so many unanswered questions and I'm terrified as to when and how I will achieve those answers.

~

"Right, I think it's safe to say that we have no further concerns here," the nurse tells me as she prepares my discharge forms. I am given a lecture on how to look after myself when I leave hospital, followed by the warning signs I should look out for.

Nick still has not appeared and a part of me is disappointed. I quickly shake the feeling; I shouldn't have even expected that he would have showed up. After all, I did push him away. Still, if he does love me as he says he does, surely he would have been here? I sigh to myself and thank the nurse for her time.

I grab my phone, the only thing I came into the hospital with, along with my discharge papers and make my way over to Katie.

"Hey, I'm off now, thank god! I hope you heal quickly. I would love to keep in touch?" Katie beams up at me and motions towards the pad of paper and pen resting on the table. I pick it up and she reels off her phone number. I tear the paper from the pad and fold it, placing it into my jacket pocket. Katie and I exchange smiles and 'goodbyes' before I head towards the exit of this stifling hot ward. I keep my head down as I power my phone on. As I look up, I see Nick hovering at the end of the corridor. Time stands still and I blink just in case I have suddenly started to hallucinate. He strides towards me. I swallow, trying to unstick my tongue from the roof of my dry mouth.

"Hey, you got everything? My Uncle is waiting in the car downstairs for us." I really don't think I can face Nick's Uncle right now. What do I say? How do I act? Will he speak to me first? I have far too many questions, once again they will remain unanswered.

"Um, yeah I'm all good. I didn't come in with anything besides my phone..." I trail off as I realise Nick will clock that I deliberately ignored his text from last night.

"Okay cool. I made your bed for you this morning so you can rest as soon as we get back home. I must admit I did sleep in your bed last night. I was lost without you." My mouth falls open at Nick's admission. I'm slightly peeved at his choice of the word 'home'. I am still certain that I will never see it as home again. For now, it will have to be. I am exhausted, only managing an hour of shuteye last night. A small part of my inner woman grins at the thought of Nick sleeping in my bed. I hope he is hurting, now he may just understand that nothing in this world goes without consequence. Keeping such a secret from me has caught up with him.

We make it out of the hospital and the fresh air is so welcoming. My sides are still immensely sore so I cannot gulp in the air as greedily as I would have liked to. Still, small breaths in do the trick.

Nick's Uncle remains silent as we both climb into the back of his jeep. I glance up into the rear-view mirror and nearly catch Sal's eye. He looks away as hastily as he can manage without looking suspicious. He gives me and Nick a quick nod. It is evident that the drive back will be undertaken in silence, for which I am relieved.

~

We pull back up to the house and all three of us exit the car as silently as we can manage. Nick makes his way around to me, putting his hand out for me. I brush him off. I do not need his help. I notice Sal give Nick a sly glance, obviously picking up on my dismissive behaviour.

I head straight for the stairs, not looking back at either man. I know I should thank Sal for the ride home from the hospital, but I feel as if I have lost the capability to speak.

True to his word, my bed is impeccably made up and the books I had carelessly left laying out have been stacked neatly. I make a quick mental note to catch up with my Social Studies and Math Tutors. I have no idea when I will go back to College, but the sooner will be better. I need some normality back in my life. I need to text Sarah; I'm slightly wounded that I haven't heard from her yet. I guess Nick hasn't text her to tell her what happened. Typical.

My bed looks beyond inviting but I know I won't be left to sleep until some issues are put to bed. Ironic that.

Nick stands in the doorway, his hands shoved deep into the pockets of his jeans. He looks at his feet. I keep staring, I just can't seem to help myself. Yes, he has been a massive pain in the arse, but it doesn't mean he is not still physically attractive. Nick finally meets my wandering eyes and I blush, caught in the act. Apparently, Nick takes that as an invitation to enter my room, closing the door shut behind him.

I am trying so hard to put distance between us, but these four walls suddenly seem to be closing in, pushing us closer together. Nick is now directly in front of me, I raise my hand asking him to stop. Nick does stop but he is far too close for my liking. I do owe it to him to hear him out. I'm just terrified of the answer. I moved myself backwards until I feel the bed behind me. I signal to Nick to come and join me. He obliges, quite willingly I might add. It must be torture for him, to have me this close yet so far.

"So, where do we start? Please tell me everything. At least everything that you know." My voice comes out pleading. Nick seems shocked that I have finally broken the silence. I'm sure he thought that he would be the one to break it.

"Okay. Please hear me out though. Promise you won't be running off or doing anything to harm yourself again?" I'm not sure if he's trying to be funny or not. I'm certainly in no state to be running anywhere. Hobble, yes. Run, no. Whatever I'm told, I will just have to deal with. Whether I like it or not.

"Okay, so my Uncle came over that afternoon. He told me that he knew instantly you are Martha's Daughter from photographs Martha had shown him. He thought that by telling me, I would be able to break it to you slowly, rather than you accidentally stumbling across your Mum in some way. You must know just how sorry I am. I couldn't find any way to tell you. I couldn't do that to you, I knew how much it would break your heart. Now I know that by keeping it from you for that time, I broke your heart anyway. I can only beg you to forgive me. Please?" I appreciate Nick's honesty, but it still does not answer the most important, burning question.

"Nick... Why though? Why did she do it?" I lock eyes with Nick. He looks lost.

"I honestly don't know Josie. I wish I did; I want to give you the answers you deserve. My Uncle and I were talking last night, we agreed it is best that Martha... I mean your Mum, tells you everything herself." I nod slowly at Nick. I believe that he doesn't know anything else. The air around us is tense, neither of us knowing what to do or say next. Nick's hand creeps closer to mine, finally settling on top of my own hand. I'm too confused to retaliate so I allow it to sit there for a while.

Nick's eyes are searching mine, trying to decipher my feelings. Before I can really grasp what is happening, Nick is leaning towards me. Panic rises in my chest, I'm not ready for this just yet.

"Nick, stop. Please just allow me to process everything. Maybe we can talk tomorrow, but for now I would really love some time for myself." It's only just gone Midday, but I need to sleep for a few hours at least. I hope to evade Nick and his Uncle Sal at dinner tonight. I think I may even take myself out of the house for a bit, a dinner date with myself... that doesn't actually sound so bad.

"You had a whole night to yourself in that ward. It killed me to leave you there, but you insisted. You cannot make me leave you again!" I'm unsure if Nick meant to raise his voice to me. I can't help but feel he is being selfish here.

"In a ward, Nick. A. Ward. It wasn't exactly a Spa Resort, was it?" I'm so proud of myself for keeping my cool through my statement. I usually suck at sarcasm but that one paid off well.

Nick looks at me in utter amazement before shaking his head and standing up. As he reaches the door, he turns back to me as if he is about to say something. He stutters but raises his hand in the air, balling his fist. Nick leaves my room, making as bold of a statement as he can by slamming the door closed behind him.

Chapter 4, Nick:

I rush into my room and slam the door. My Uncle must be wondering what the hell is going on, I've managed to successfully slam two doors in the space of a minute. I'm beyond pissed off. She isn't even trying; she's just acting as if she is the only person in the world that has ever received some sort of shock to the system.

Maybe I am being too harsh on her. Fuck knows how I would react if the roles were reversed and it was Josie keeping that sort of thing from me.

I'm lost, it's still so early in the day. The thought of making small talk with my Uncle fills me with dread. He'll just talk shit about business and what book is bringing in the most royalties at the moment. I would rather stab my eye out with a fork. I need to see Sam.

Pulling my phone from the back pocket of my jeans (a habit I just cannot break out of), I scroll to Sam's name and press the green telephone icon. As the line rings, I pick at the skin around my fingers. Sam's voice greets me a little too eagerly.

"Nick my Sonnn! What's going on Man, where in the hell have you been? Josie been keeping you busy, eh?" I can hear his cockiness down the phone. He thinks he's a right funny fucker. Shame I'm about to make him feel like a colossal twat.

"Hey Man, Me and Josie aren't actually great. I told her." I hear Sam's breath catch in his throat out of amazement. I'm sure he didn't expect me to actually go through with it. Especially as I was acting like a wimp when we were discussing it. Sam thought it was the right thing to do, I disagreed. Look who was right all along. Oh, me! What a surprise.

"Shit... How did she take it? Stupid question I know." Sam has no idea.

"Well, she was hurt... I don't think she will ever trust me again. She was hit by a car." I hear Sam take a lungful of air, gasping in surprise at the news.

"WHAT?! YOU SHOULD HAVE LED WITH THAT. JESUS CHRIST NICK!" I pull the phone away from my ear before Sam makes me deaf. I should have known better than to call him. I'm only just realising how not in the mood I am for his dramatics. I've sown the seed now though. If I do not continue to explain, Sam will just show up here.

"Yeah, Martha... her mum, showed up here just as she found out. Josie ran from the house and straight into the road. She's okay, sort of. Broken ribs and concussion. She's bruised quite badly in other various places. They kept her in overnight but she's home now. I've tried to make things right Sam... it's over though." My voice cracks and hot, angry tears begin to well up in my eyes. I feel so weak.

"Oh mate, I am so sorry. Just think, what you have revealed to her is massive. She has spent the past three -nearly four- years of her life grieving someone she thought to be gone for good. Not just anyone Nick but her own Mother. She was forced to live with her Stepmother and Father who treated her like pure and utter shit. Now, combine all those things together and imagine how you would feel. You're lucky that she is still there. I feel like if this were Sarah and not Josie, I would have been dumped on my arse by now." Sam attempts to make light of the situation, laughing at his comment. I am lucky, I guess, that Josie is still here. Realistically I know its only becase she has nowhere else to go. I feel awful even thinking that. Josie will always have a place here; it infuriates me to think that she will want to go elsewhere. We have not discussed it yet so I'm not sure what her intentions are. Does she want to stay here? There is no possible way she would want to go back to her Stepmother and Dad, is there?

"I guess you are right. I am trying to put myself in her shoes, I really am. She's just so closed off from me and it's killing me inside. Are you free? I could use some company." I ask Sam, knowing that he will always make the time for me as I will for him. That's just what friends do.

"Sure, Man come to mine if you like. Don't worry, Sarah isn't here. We can spend time apart." Sam laughs to himself, as if I really care about the amount of time they spend together.

"Alright, I'll see you in a bit." I hang up the phone and start to get myself ready. The weather has taken a turn for the worst, rain pelting against my window. I need a car. Usually I would walk to Sam's no problem, not in this weather though. I'll have to fork out for a bloody taxi. Car hunting can wait for a bit though, it's the least of my worries on my ever-growing list of shit that needs doing in my life.

Chapter 5, Josie:

I wake with a start, pain shooting up my side. I snap my hand over my ribs and attempt to take some deep breaths. Normally when I am in pain, I end up holding my breath as I ride out the tidal wave. I need some painkillers. Switching on the lamp, I shift my eyes to both beside tables thinking that Nick may have put some aside for me. I am mistaken.

I sigh, knowing I will have to swallow my pride and make my way downstairs to grab some. The way me and Nick left things is not exactly ideal. I know if I run into him that he will be off with me and I cannot deal with his attitude right now.

I manage to make it to the bottom of the stairs, is going downstairs supposed to make you this out of breath?

Nick's Uncle Sal is sat in the lounge, his nose in a book. His glasses are perched on the end of his nose. I try to remain silent as I pass him towards the kitchen, unfortunately I am unsuccessful as his eyes snap away from the pages and towards me. He clears his throat far too audibly, evidence that he still feels uncomfortable in my presence. He gives me a quick nod, shoving his glasses back to where they should be sitting on his face. I reciprocate the nod and amble my way towards the kitchen.

"Nick's popped over to Sam's for a bit in case you were looking for him." The sound of Sal's voice makes me jump; I was sure we were just going to continue our silence. I wish I had the guts to tell him my thoughts on his statement. I could not care less where Nick is. Well, that isn't necessarily true, I do miss him so I can't help the pang of disappointment that creeps into the pit of my stomach from not seeing him. It took all my self-restraint not to go after Nick when he stormed from my bedroom. The light flickers on in the kitchen and I head straight to where the medicines are kept. Popping two Ibuprofen out of their blisters, I take a glass and fill it with cold water. I hate swallowing pills. When I was a bit younger, ten or so, my Mum would have to stand with me as I took them otherwise, I would just give up and chuck them away. I fill my mouth with water and gulp down the small, white painkillers. The water is so refreshing, and I end up filling the glass again as soon as I finish downing the first.

I feel so alone right now, not just because Nick is not here but in general... I haven't heard from anyone. Not Maxie, not Sarah, just no one... Tears begin to prick my eyes. I decide that calling Sarah would more than likely help me. I need to hear her voice. I need to unload everything. Sarah, better than anyone, listens to everything. She never judges and will always wait a few seconds after anything I say, just in case there is more to come.

I refill the glass to take back to my bedroom with me. Nick's Uncle decides to keep his eyes on his book this time as I walk back past him.

As I enter my room, my phone lights up. I pick it up and set the water down in its place. I read the small preview of the text on my screen. I don't recognise the number but instinctively, I know who it is. It's the same number that had flashed onto my screen the night me and Nick ate ourselves into a pizza coma. I wish I could just be given some space to figure out this shit. I still haven't sat down and really thought about everything. I know when I finally do, I'll fall apart. It's a lot to throw at someone. Not even the world's strongest person would be able to handle it.

'Josie please, we need to talk. If you just answer me, I can explain everything.' She's out of her damn mind. Where was she four years ago when I needed her? Where was she on the nights I cried for her or when I would stand in an isolated area and scream my pain out as loud as possible?

Where was she when my Stepmother was slapping me and draining me of my self-esteem? She was out there just shacking up with Nick's Uncle. Both of them should be ashamed of themselves. Sal's reaction to seeing me for the first time makes sense now. He knew instantly who I was. I should have called him out on his shit back then. Instead, I was just hurt, thinking that Nick's Uncle had taken an instant dislike to me. I curse at fate for landing me directly in the life of Nicholas Peters. Fate could have chosen to place me directly into some other poor sap's life but no, it had to be fucking Nick Peters...

~

"Josie! Oh my goodness I have been so worried about you! How are you?" I feel instant relief at the sound of Sarah's voice. It took me a while to finally pluck up the courage to call her. I tried reasoning with myself that I shouldn't be mad at her.

"Hey, I'm okay. How have you been? Did Nick tell you about the last couple of days?" I really hope he has. If not, this phone call may last the whole night.

"I am so good! No, what's happened? I know he's with Sam at the moment, but Sam hasn't told me shit. He wouldn't dare whilst he's around Nick." Sarah laughs to herself, completely oblivious to how much of a car crash (literally) my life has been the past week.

"How much time do you have?" My voice cracks and I kick myself for constantly being a wreck.

"I have all the time in world. Talk to me, it sounds like you need to get it all out." She's right. I really need to get it all out but where do I start with it all? Oh, you know, Nick lied to me and made you guys keep a massive secret from me. Turns out I was living in a house where the secret was right under my bloody nose and my Mum isn't dead! My supposed to be dead Mum rocks up to the house just as I unravel everything, and I get hit by a car! It sounds crazy when I say it to myself so fuck knows what Sarah will make of it.

"Why did you say what you did to me? Remember when you said I would always have a place with you if things don't work out between Nick and I. Tell me truthfully." I am begging Sarah to be truthful with me. It's already a blow that she would keep it from me to protect Nick when she is supposed to be my friend.

"Um, well, sometimes things just don't work out. I would never have you go back to your Stepmother and Dad." There it is, I should've known she wouldn't tell me.

"So, it isn't anything to do with how I would feel if I were to find out something. I don't know, like my Mum being alive and Nick knowing?" I hear Sarah gasp. She knows she's been caught out.

"Josie, please hear me out. When Sam told me, he said that Nick would be telling you that evening, I thought that you needed to know someone had your back. I waited for the phone call, but it never came. I knew Nick would chicken out. I planned to tell you when I next saw you, but you never showed to college. Sam and I had no idea what was going on. How are you feeling about every-thing? Ignore that, it's a stupid question." Sarah sounds so pan-icked that I just can't find it in myself to be cross with her. At the end of the day, Sarah was placed into an awkward situation and I must put myself in her shoes. How would I feel if it were Sarah in my situation? I wouldn't be able to tell my best friend and watch the pain spread across her face. I guess I understand.

"It's okay, relax. It isn't your fault; you didn't make the situation what it is. I know why you chose not to tell me. I would not be able to tell you if the roles were reversed. I really do not know how I feel. I was so shocked to see her standing there. I was sure it was a dream, a crazy and fucked up one at that. I ran from the house and I was hit by a car." Sarah makes a sound between a screech and a gasp. If she were standing in front of me, she would have her hand over her mouth and her bright eyes would be open as wide as possible.

"JESUS! Are you badly hurt?"

"No, not badly. I have a few broken ribs and I had a concussion.

They kept me in for the night to make sure there wasn't anything going on they should be concerned about. My ribs will take, at the least, six months to heal. I can't do sports or lift anything too heavy but there isn't much you can do for broken ribs really. I've just been resting since getting home, well… back to Nick's. I don't think this is 'home' anymore." I bite my cheek to keep the tears from spilling down my cheeks.

"Oh, you poor soul. If you need anything then just holler at your girl. The offer of staying with me is still on the table, you know that right?" I do know that. It seriously is something I am considering. I love Nick. I adore Nick, but will this distance between us ever become easier? I know I am the one putting the distance between us, but I can't have him thinking that keeping things from me is okay. A relationship is built on trust. If you cannot trust your significant other, then really what is the use of fooling yourself that it will work? I need to stay here until I can figure my head out. I mentally pat myself on the back for never moving into Nick's bedroom like he wanted me to. Having my own room means I can evade Nick and his Uncle if I need to, especially since there is a lock on the door. I know with Nick's temper, he could easily break his way in, but I know he respects me enough to avoid doing so.

"Thank you. I know the offer is still there and I really appreciate it. Would you mind keeping the offer open for a little while please? I can't deal with the stress of moving again but when I can, I will leave here." I hope the words are more convincing than my voice sounds.

"Sure girl. Do you think you and Nick will ever patch things up?" I stare at the floor. I would love for me and Nick to go back to the bliss we were in before all this bullshit happened. It only feels like yesterday that I was lying in Nick's arms after we made love. After he told me how much he loves me and how I am the first girl he has ever loved. I believed him then, and I still do now.

"I really don't know. Maybe, I just need to take things one day at a time though." I fear if too much happens too fast, I will truly lose sight of myself. I already feel like I am living someone else's life. "Anyway, how are you and Sam? Have you been up to much?"

Sarah spends the next five minutes telling me that her and Sam are basically joined at the hip. Knowing me too well, she promises she will send over the work I have missed out on as my tutors are yet to respond to my emails. I thank her and she laughs before responding "only you can think of college at a time like this." I tell her that work will distract me from everything going on around me. To be honest, I have been so into my own head that the world could stop spinning and I would be oblivious.

Sarah and I end the call just as I hear the front door closing. As quick as my ribs and bruises will allow, I go to my bedroom door and quickly turn the lock. The last thing I want right now is for Nick to try and force a conversation on me, especially as my conversation with Sarah has drained the smidge of energy I did have.

Sure enough, my door handle is pressed down, and I hear Nick attempt to budge the door open. My name is spoken through the door in questioning, Nick wondering if I am asleep. I wonder if his Uncle told him of our earlier encounter. I remain silent. I feel immature doing so, after all he just wants to make sure I am okay. I hear him huff and step away from my door. I release the breath I didn't realise I was holding. I'm secretly pissed off that he can still affect me despite what he did to me.

I need some music; it always makes me feel calmer. When I lived with my Stepmother and Dad, music was my metaphorical hero, carrying me away from the sounds of raised voices and harsh words. Between music and books, I survived. If the two things did not exist, I feel that I would have dead long ago. I know that sounds completely dramatic but it's the God honest truth. I look down at the scars on my arms, proof that I survived a traumatic past. The worst scars run the length of my arm. Maxie found me and I was rushed to hospital. I blamed it on bullying, fooling the doctors who questioned me. I was appointed a therapist, fat lot of use that was. I ended up lying my way through the sessions and I was discharged earlier than I should have been. I know it would have helped to be truthful, to tell the bearded man sat across from me that I was facing daily nightmares at home, but I just couldn't. My first ever therapist was an older woman, she did not have a single thing out of place. Her skirts were knee length with not a single wrinkle. Her make-up was sharp. She reminded me of a strict schoolteacher. She tricked me into believing I was in safe hands. I had told her all about my Mum passing away (or so I thought) before telling her about my home life. As soon as she muttered "well maybe you are just a difficult child", I had left the small room and never returned. I was stunned that the blame had been placed on me, like I had asked my Stepmother to hate me. My teenage years continued like this for some time. I would self-harm, it would be uncovered accidentally, and I would be appointed more therapy. I thought I had found solace in Roberta Green, but it turns out she was more twisted and untrustworthy than any other therapist I had dealt with.

I cross the floor of my bedroom and dig through my handbag for my earphones. I spend a couple of minutes untangling the mess they have somehow got themselves in to before plugging them into my phone. I scroll through my usual playlist to find the loudest track I have. I finally find the perfect one 'Your Betrayal by Bullet For My Valentine', how apt that song is to my current situation. I turn the volume all the way up, ignoring the warning on my phone about high volumes damaging your hearing. After the things I have heard as of late, lack of hearing sounds more like a blessing.

My eardrums vibrate as I lay back on the bed and allow the music to consume me.

Chapter 6, Nick:

Being in Sam's company for a few hours really helped to heal some of my damaged soul. That was, until I glanced over his shoulder to a text from his beau: *'Just spoke to Josie, poor lamb is so upset with everything. I feel awful for not just telling her. I'm sure Nick probably didn't break the new in the softest way. She is considering moving in with me. Don't tell him.'* I cleared my throat to show Sam that I had just read every word of that awful text message.

Sam has always been my fire extinguisher. When it comes to Josie, I am always ablaze. A gigantic fucking fire, threatening to ruin everything around me unless I am quickly dealt with. Sam assured me that there will be more to the text, so not to overthink things. The red fury that clouds my vision made it difficult for me to think straight.

To no surprise, Josie's bedroom door is locked. I wish she wouldn't shut me out. Clearly her Mother or Father had some sort of stubborn temperament, now passed on to their stubborn arse of a Daughter. We need to talk in depth about the future. Will the future be ours? How would I feel if she found someone else? The image in my mind is sickening. Josie is mine. I always thought that was a stupid expression, labelling a person as 'yours'. People aren't property. Josie has changed so many of my beliefs and morals. She is mine and I, hers. She has all of me: body, soul and mind. I wonder if she feels the same way about me. Am I merely a 'boyfriend' to her? Labels have never bothered me, before Josie I had never even entertained the idea of a 'girlfriend'. Josie is so much more to me than just a stereotypical label. She is my world, heart and soul all rolled into one. Without her, I feel like I would be unable to breathe. I shudder at the memory of being without her last night, remembering how it felt to be so alone and empty, consumed by my guilt and forced to listen to the evil voice in my head.

My bedroom feels as if it has doubled in size. I feel like a tiny speck of dust in the middle of this vast room. I wish I had the balls to just drag Josie kicking and screaming from her room to be here with me. I have always loved the company of me, myself and I, so why do I suddenly reject the feeling so readily? I allow myself to fall back onto the soft mound of duvet. There is no way I'll be able to sleep just yet. I could do some coursework, but I could also shoot myself, I know which one I'd rather do. The anger at Sarah's text has yet to dissipate and I am surprised I have kept it so controlled since getting home. My wardrobe is still scattered all over my floor and my gym shorts catch my eye. I suppose a run might do me some good. It's been a while since I used the gym. I rise from my bed slowly, padding over to the Mount Everest of clothes. I pull the gym shorts out, causing the other clothes piled on top to come crashing down. I unbutton my jeans and peel them off, hurling them on to my bed. I still have so much laundry to do but for now those jeans will be good enough for anther days' worth of wear. I know if Josie could see the state of this room compared to her own, she would be running around like a lunatic straightening everything up. I would stop her, which would drive her crazy and we would collapse on to my bed, laughing. We would make love and I would come undone at the sound of my name falling from her lips, tidying my room now being the farthest thing from her thoughts. If only a daydream could be pulled from one's head and instantly made a reality.

I leave my bedroom with my phone and headphones in hand. I stop outside of Josie's door out of habit and hear her soft breathing. I cannot tell if she's awake or asleep, but I guess it isn't any of my business. I pad downstairs, the house cloaked in darkness. I flick on the hall light and the space is instantly lit; my Uncle must have changed the bulb at some point. I check the lounge and kitchen, but I am alone. My Uncle's coat isn't hanging on it's usual peg and his keys are also missing. My Uncle is very ritualistic in where he hangs things. A glance out of the lounge window confirms that he has took off again, fuck knows where to or how long for.

I open the door to the basement and make my way down, the smell of polished wood hitting my nostrils. The basement looks so clean. It can't have been used much recently.

I select the running machine in the middle of the room and plug my music in to my ears before booting up the machine. I quickly crank up the speed. My feet hit the belt over and over, slamming away some of the tension that rests heavily on my chest. I had some anger management classes a while back now and my counsellor advised me to commence exercise if possible whenever I begin to feel the usual anger making its way through my body. I took this advice when the classes were still fresh in my mind but in recent years, that advice has just gone over my head. The feeling I am experiencing right now reminds me of why exercise helps to rationalise my emotions. I feel euphoric, my heart hammering away in a welcoming way. I am already sweating, and I feel the usual burn creeping into my leg muscles. I really should have stretched before stepping on to the treadmill. *Little too late for that now Nick.*

I am so lost in my own head and in the lyrics of the music artist blessing my ears, that I have no idea I am no longer alone in the room. The floor is so shiny that I spot the movement of someone behind me. I quickly pull the stop cord, allowing the belt to slow enough before I step off and look into the bewildered face of Josie. She's stood with her arms crossed over her chest; her eyes fixated on me. She looks amused at the state I am in. I know I need a shower, so I keep the distance between us. I want to walk over to her and cup her beautiful face. I want to beg her not to leave me again. All I can do is gawp at her, amazed that she is stood before my very eyes.

I notice her chest rising and falling quicker than is normal. She's deep in thought, all the while keeping her eyes fixed on mine. She pulls her bottom lip in between her teeth and I lose it. Striding over to her, I place both hands either side of her face, relishing in the feeling of being able to hold her again. I sigh in relief when she does not push me away.

I'm treading carefully, not wanting to make a singular wrong move. I am waiting for her cue.

She takes a step towards me; she is clearly as apprehensive as I am. I have always been one to just take what I want. If I do that with her, is that selfish? Fuck it. I lower my mouth down to hers and press my lips against hers. She makes the smallest moan and it ignites every sense in my body. I have missed her so much. She reciprocates my actions and I find myself back on the porch when we kissed for the first ever time. She was nervous, but her eager mouth on mine distracted away from that fact. Just like then, her mouth is desperate. Our kiss is heated, and I have to restrain myself from grabbing her and pulling her flush to me, knowing how fragile she is at the moment. I love this girl with every inch of myself. I feel the love deep in my core, in my bones. She doesn't seem to care how sweaty I am as she wraps her arms around my torso. As quick as her lips had met mine, they are suddenly removed, and I wince. She looks like heaven, her swollen lips shine in the low light. I am aware of how I must be looking at her. She keeps her arms around me as she places her head on my chest. I don't say anything, I just hug her back as delicately as I can manage. When I was ranting to Sam about Josie's distance and how it has been killing me slowly, Sam had told me to "wait for her to come to you and when she does, just be there for her." In this moment, that is precisely what I am doing. I am being there for her, telling her without words that in this moment, she is safe in my arms.

Josie sighs into my chest and I chuckle, causing her head to move along with the movements my chuckle causes in my chest. I have missed this attitude. I know all is not forgiven and, in a moment, I will have lost her again. I am okay with this, I have her for now and I know to cherish it before it is ripped away from my grasp all over again.

Josie finally drops her arms from around me and steps backwards. I decide not to speak until she has, I am just renowned for saying the wrong thing at the wrong time. Don't mess up this moment Nicholas.

"I'm sorry, I don't want to give you the wrong idea." The look that creeps on to my face at her comment is one of rejection. Is she regretting it? "I don't regret any part of it, I just don't want you to feel that you can do something like that to me and I will just come running back." I swear that girl is inside my head, able to read every thought. It's quite haunting sometimes.

"It's okay. I will always be here for you, whatever you need. If kissing and hugging me is what brings you comfort right now, then so be it." I laugh slightly so as not to sound sarcastic. Josie grins back at me and I relax myself slightly. At least we are not screaming at each other.

"Are you going to stay with Sarah?" My mouth jumps into action before my brain has any time to catch up. Fuck sake Nick... I knew I would end up saying something without putting thought into it first. Josie looks slightly hurt by my sudden outburst. She either thinks Sarah told me about their conversation or she thinks I want her gone from here. The latter of the two could be farther from the truth. I never want her to leave but she's slowly becoming more distant from me.

"No. I told Sarah I would think about it. I just do not want the stress of moving right now, but when I am able to, I more than likely will be moving to Sarah's. Do you want me to go?" Josie's words slice through me. I get the sudden urge to drop to my knees and beg her to never leave me. My pride constantly gets in the way of doing the right thing.

"I saw a text she sent to Sam; Sarah would never willingly tell me anything you guys discuss. I am sure she dislikes me, and she has every reason to. Josie please never say things like that. Of course

I do not want you to go. I wish you would never go. Can you not see how hard I am trying?" A small frown has made its way across Josie's forehead and I know she is gearing up to shout all sorts of things at me. I deserve every word. I will allow her to say all she needs to, but I am beginning to become defensive of myself. I never asked my Uncle to unveil the truth to me that should have been uncovered to her. I have stayed by her side through all this mess and I intend to stay. I want to help her figure this out, but she makes it impossible by shoving me away.

"Wow, you really are so narcistic Nick. How hard you are trying? You must be joking. You have not tried at all. You have the nerve to make me feel like I should just welcome you back with open arms. You knew about this FOR DAYS but chose to only tell me when I spoke up in front of your Mother. Even then, you were angry with me for calling you out on your bullshit. Tell me truthfully, if I had never suspected anything was being kept from me, would you have told me willingly?" Josie reminds me of an angry cat. Her hackles are raised, and she has made herself taller to appear more intimidating.

"Truthfully... Eventually, yes I would have. I knew it would break your heart and we had just fallen for each other. You know I never used to date anyone and suddenly you fall... No, you crash, into my life. Suddenly I am having to try not to break a girl's heart. Yes, I know I am a dick. I treated women like shit. Can you not imagine how hard it is to go from being selfish to caring about someone else's feelings? You wouldn't know though; you have never been selfish. Your life has been full of pleasing others. That is why you feel things so deeply." My words resonate through her and I can tell from the tears pouring down her face. I know she is hurt but if we are laying our cards out on the table, then I will be as truthful as I possibly can. In most romance novels and films, there is always that one stereotypical 'bad boy' that entices the innocent girl to fall for him as a joke, only to find himself falling madly in love with her. I feel like I am this stereotypical boy and we are in our own romance novel. Josie is the innocent girl, she has never even so much as hurt a fly in her life, yet she has always been hurt by so many other people. Her Mum, Dad, Stepmother and that flowery therapist woman have all been contributors to her heartbreak. I know I should add myself to this list, but Josie is right. I am a narcissist. I wanted to shield her from the truth, even if it was not my truth to be keeping. I am also aware that the 'bad boys' from novels always have a reputation of being heartbreakers. It isn't a path I wanted to walk. I got off on being able to make girls swoon over me, but I was also doing it to be noticed. My Mum had pretty much abandoned me, and my Uncle was (and still isn't) ever home, his publishing business coming first in his life. He could never deal with the hormonal teenage boy that was suddenly thrust at arm's length to him. I never blamed him or resented him for that. He looked after me, always making sure I had money for food or filling up the house with food when he did come home briefly. I would never admit it to him, but I always wished he would adopt me. My own parents being able to abandon me so easily still weighs heavily on my chest whenever I let my mind wander off to that dark place. I guess that by using girls, I felt less lonely. For one short moment, someone wanted me, even if it was for their own gratification.

"Thank you for being honest with me. I just wish you hadn't treated me like a weak, pathetic little girl. I do not need protecting. I have always got myself through the worst things in my life by myself. So, there was no need to try and protect my heart. I don't have one anymore. My heart was taken from me as soon as I moved in with my Stepmother and Dad. I am numb to most things now. We could have sat and gone through everything together. I would never have run, and we wouldn't be here like this now," Josie gestures to the space between us. "Keeping it from me is what hurts me the most. I thought I had left the horrible parts of my life behind. I thought the Devil had finally listened to me and he was finally accepting my soul, in return that I would be able to have a normal life. It now just feels like the Devil laughed at me. You are right, I have never been selfish. The first time I was selfish was when I ignored my Stepmother and spent the afternoon in your bed. Oh my god... Did you hold off telling me so you could carry on having sex with me?" If the conversation was not as serious as it is, I would have laughed at that comment. Judging by the horrified look on her face she is not joking. Why would she think that low of me? What more can I do to prove to this girl that I have given up everything for her?

"You have got to be fucking joking... How and why could you think that?!" The control I had has now disappeared. I have begun to speak through gritted teeth, and I feel the familiar bubble of anger rising. Josie does not look in the least bit intimidated, standing her ground. I never want her to fear me, but she can't say something so degrading to me. I won't let that shit just slide. She opens her mouth, but I raise my hand to continue.

"I have given up so much for you. I took you in when you had nowhere else to go. I have stood by you through all of this. I have kept myself as far away from you, against my better judgement, when you have asked me for space. It is killing me right now to finally be so close to you but have you so far at the same time. WHAT DO YOU WANT FROM ME?" Josie jumps at my raised voice. She has apparently moved past tears straight to anger. The speed at which her chest is rising and falling must be causing her significant pain, but she doesn't once wince as her eyes burn into mine.

"Whatever Nick. I would have found somewhere else to go. You can continue to play hero on your own, I am over this discussion. I don't have the strength to go in circles with you all night long." She turns her back to me and begins to head towards the stairs. I know it's wrong but the sight of her walking away from me fuels my anger further and I already know that the next words from my mouth will be hurtful.

"You had nowhere else to go. You had no one else." She stops and spins around with a sickening speed, steadying herself against the wall. In a flash, she is in front of me and I am being shoved with a force I never imagined could come from someone of Josie's build.

"YOU FUCKER! I HAVE PEOPLE... I HAVE PEOPLE." She continues her shoving as she lies to herself. As her hands come back up from her sides to continue her assault on my chest, I grab her wrists. She is like an angry Tasmanian devil as she fights to get out of my grip. I beg her to stop fighting me, worrying that she'll cause herself an injury: a new one or an addition to her existing ones. She doesn't relent and I end up giving her the same bear hug that my Uncle had ended up giving me only yesterday evening. History sure has a way of replaying itself.

Finally, Josie stills in my arms and shakes from her sobs. I slide us both down the wall we ended up against until we are both seated on the floor. I wrap my legs around her until she is cocooned by both my legs and arms. I hold her as her hot tears slide down her cheeks and drip onto my arms. She finally gives in and rests her head on my chest in the way I love. I kiss the top of her head and she tenses from the affection. How we have managed to keep our distance for this long is beyond me. I knew I should've barged her door open earlier. I have missed her but slowly she is coming back to me... I hope.

Chapter 7, Josie:

I fought hard against Nick until I had no more fight left in me. He said the most hurtful things he could but as odd as it sounds, it was actually nice to hear them. The words made me cringe but I felt something, finally I have been able to cry. My chest hurts the most that it has since the accident but I know it's worth it for the pressure being expelled from me now.

I sit in between Nick's legs, his arms wrapped around me holding me safe. We haven't said anything for a couple of minutes but the silence is welcoming for once. For once it isn't deafening.

It was wrong of me to kiss Nick. It was wrong of me to even come down here. I heard the sound of the treadmill thumping at the bottom of the house. Sal had left so I knew it could only be Nick down here. The blasting music had soothed my soul in a way that only music can. I felt a new found confidence as I made my way down the stairs towards my hero... An odd hero dressed in gym shorts and sweating like a cow in a slaughterhouse, but a hero none the less. I never realised what my life was lacking until Nick. I know there's a way for us to work through the looming issue but I just don't know how.

Nick places the most delicate kiss on the top of my head. I tilt my head up to look directly into his eyes. The green eyes that stare back at me are lit up with intensity. He looks both worried and curious. Nick studies my face, his eyes flicking back and forth. The pair of lips I am so desperate to kiss again are puckered in the cutest way, a small pout forming as he continues his investigation of my face. The way he looks at me is the look you would give someone you knew you'd never see again. He's soaking in all of my features as if I'll leave this room and never look back. Maybe that's the right thing to do? Spending the day alone has left me wondering many things. What would it be like to just disappear? To run away and never look back. To go somewhere where no one knows your name, face or past.

Nick removes one hand from my waist and lifts it up to my face in his usual fashion. I know where this is going and there is no way I am stopping it. Our lips collide and my moan gives me away. Nick's thumb swipes away the tears from my cheek. When I'm in his hands, I always feel like a porcelain doll, he is so gentle and careful with how he handles me. I usually love it but right now I'm finding it infuriating. I don't want to be treated carefully, not right now. I push my lips and body further into Nick's. I ignore the pain that shoots through me, knowing if I make the pain known that Nick will cease all action, and that is not what I want. He doesn't deepen the kiss as I want him to so I move my hand to the nape of his neck, forcing him closer. Nick moans and pulls his lips away to speak my name. I shake my head at him.

"Don't worry about hurting me, I'll be okay. Please just kiss me like you mean it. Kiss me like you'll never see me again." Nick pulls away with force. A deep scowl across his face and the green in his eyes fading to black.

"Don't say shit like that to me!" Before we have a chance to get into another shouting match, Nick crashes his lips back onto mine and finally kisses me with the force I have been wishing for. He moves his lips from mine and trails small kisses down my neck, I feel the blood rushing up through my dermis as his lips pull on the delicate skin of my neck. I moan, earning a small smile from his dreamy lips. The euphoria I feel in this moment is indescribable. I feel empowered and alive all at once.

I twist my body from Nick's and he pulls away looking hurt. I was only twisting my body so that I can face him, but he must think I am having second thoughts. Not a chance. We will be finishing what we started.

I place my legs on either side of his body and he shuffles into me hastily, not wanting to be away from me a second longer. I feel the pull between us. It's something I can only describe as a strong magnetic pull, Nick being my magnet. We resume what we started, my lips eager on his and his lips just as eager on mine. His hands grip the bottom of the baggy T- shirt I threw on before making me way to him earlier, and he lifts it over my head, groaning as we break contact yet again. As Nick drops the material beside me, I watch as his eyes take in the sight of my chest. It's such an invasive stare that I blush and begin to move my arms up to cover myself. I didn't want to risk a bra in case my ribs protested so I had decided that the baggiest shirt would be best. Nick looks shocked and I realise that this is the first time since my accident that he has seen the real damage done to my body. I have deep bruising all along my left side, starting at my hip and travelling up to the side of my breast. I must look like I've been in the world's most awful fight. Nick is struggling to peel his eyes away from me and his mouth has dropped open. I flinch slightly when his fingertips begin investigating my bruises. Nick stops and I nod at him to continue, it doesn't hurt but the sudden skin on skin contact had surprised me. I was so lost in Nick's eyes that I hadn't seen his hand move to my side. I relish the feeling of his fingers on me, as much as I loved the roughness of our little make out session only minutes ago, I also love that he treats my body like it's a temple. There's a look on Nick's face that I can't make out. Shock... No, more like anger and upset. It's such a soft anger and I can't make sense of it.

"These bruises shouldn't be here. They don't belong on your body. I just want to kiss them away." Nick's voice suddenly fills the space around us, breaking through the barrier of silence we had become accustomed to. The words resonate through me, leaving me slightly breathless. Nick suddenly stands and I hold my breath, scared that he has changed his mind and my injuries have scared him off. I watch as nick stands on his tiptoes to grab some gym mats from a shelf. He gives them a quick look over before placing them down on the shiny laminate flooring. He extends an arm out to me, I stand and make my way over to him.

"Lay yourself down on the mats. I want to be on top of you." The words cause my body to ignite and I gulp in anticipation. I don't recognise the male voice that belongs to Nick. His tone has shifted from it's usual softness, to one of primality, deep and wanting. His eyes are hooded, watching my every move as I lay myself back on the mat. This is so hot. I'm trying not to make my eagerness known but as I wriggle slightly, Nick smiles. Damn, even the smile is animalistic.

Nick is above me and I watch him take his shirt off like it's the first time I've ever seen him do it. His muscles are still glistening from his recent workout. I swipe my tongue across my bottom lip, goading Nick. He seems to realise what I'm doing and winks at me, making me giggle seductively.

Nick lowers himself onto me, his legs either side of mine and his hands beside my head. I am at the stage of pleading when he dips his head down and trails small, gentle kisses along my ribs. If it were possible, I feel that his kisses would heal my bruises and breaks until I look back to my normal self. I feel his erection digging into my thigh and I raise my hips in wanting. Nick smiles into my skin, his ego inflated by my need for him. He is taking this all too slow and the suspense is killing me. Just as Nick raises himself and begins to push into me, the front door closes upstairs causing us both to raise our heads towards the direction of the noise. I hear Sal calling for Nick and I groan in frustration. If only I'd come down here sooner, we would have had our chance before being interrupted.

"I guess we can save this for later." Nick sounds apprehensive but stands anyway. You have got to be shitting me... I try to appear unaffected as I also stand. Nick has already reached the bottom of the stairs before I've even grabbed my clothes. When did my shorts come off? I must have got so lost in the moment that I didn't notice them come off. Was it me or Nick? I decide that it isn't important as I pull them back up my legs. I pull the baggy shirt back onto my body and shiver as the cool fabric touches my skin. I fold away the gym mats and stack them against the wall. I don't want to risk reaching up to the shelves to put them back in case my ribs throw a tantrum at me but I make sure they're neatly stacked. The vibrant red of the mats looks so strange against the clean contrast of the brightly lit, glossy brown laminated gym.

I hear Nick's voice, the bass of which is so high it rings off the walls. I can tell he is annoyed at being interrupted, then again so am I. I've never experienced sexual frustration before but I get it now. I get why it's a big thing. It feels awful.

I make my way slowly up the stairs, flicking off the lights as I make my way through the door and step into the hallway. I follow the voices to the lounge but stop just before I can come into view. Will it look strange if I suddenly appear but not from upstairs? Will Nick's Uncle figure out that we were just together? I realise how ridiculous that sounds. We are both consenting adults.

I step forward and stand in the doorway, the men's eyes peeling away from one another to look at me. I stand awkwardly not really knowing whether to speak or just stand there. Sal looks towards his Nephew in a manner of questioning. Nick shakes his head and I notice Sal take a deep breath, obviously planning to ignore Nick and talk to me anyway.

"Evening Josie, please come in. Sit." Something in his tone instantly makes my feet move into the room towards the sofas. I hesitantly sit, my gaze focusing in on Sal, making my point that I know he has something to tell me.

"I've been speaking to your Mum today..." Sal trails off as he notices me wince at his use of the word 'mum'. "Martha, I've been talking to Martha today. She said she sent you a text just after your accident but you haven't got back to her yet, which is understandable or course. We discussed her coming here so the two of you can talk somewhere safe. It's completely your choice. Nick here thinks it's too soon but I personally think you've had too much kept from you already." Nick hasn't looked at me yet, I know him all too well now to know that he only avoids my eyes when there is something he needs to say to me. It's the same way he acted after his Uncle left that day. The day he found out the thing that would change my life but he chose not to tell me. I keep my eyes fixed on Nick, hoping he will finally look at me. My mind is racing. I haven't received any texts as far as I'm aware. Nick was the one who bought me my phone when he was finally able to see me in the hospital. Maybe he deleted them? No. He wouldn't do that.... Would he? Is it too soon to see her? Will she tell me the full truth?

"Okay. Invite her over, but tell her she needs to be fully prepared to tell me everything." Sal visibly relaxes and nods at me with acceptance. He stands and makes his way out of the room, leaving me and Nick alone. I can't stand the tension anymore so I stand and make my way over to where Nick is sitting on the adjacent sofa. I place my hand on his thigh and squeeze reassuringly. I've come to know that when Nick is silent it's usually because his anger is bubbling up under the surface. I know that I need to extinguish the small flame before it becomes an inferno.

"Please talk to me. What's wrong?" I ask the question as silently as I can. My words cutting through the air like a knife, the tension is that thick.

"I don't want you to be hurt again. The last time you were hurt I lost you. I still haven't got you back entirely." Nick's voice is so childlike. He really means every syllable.

"Hey, look at me." Nick listens to my command and looks into my eyes. His eyes a mixture of confusion and fear. Finally, he moves his hand over mine atop his thigh.

"I need to see her; I need the closure. Maybe there's a chance that me and her can make things work again. We were practically best friends and when she died, a part of me also died. There's a slight chance that she has a pretty good explanation for what sh-"

"NO! There is never a good explanation for doing that to someone. Especially when that person is their own Daughter. I believe you should hear why just so you can rest your mind, however I do think you should just be careful." I know Nick is right. I have gone over every possible scenario in my head so it'll finally be good to hear the truth. I understand Nick feeling angry at hearing me speak in a fond manner about the woman who is my Mother, I don't really feel like I'm in control of my feelings right now.

"Thank you for being so supportive. You've been dragged into this against your choice." Before I can gauge what is happening, Nick has knelt over me, his knees either side of my thighs on the sofa. He holds my head in his hands in the way I love. He makes fleeting looks back and forth between my eyes and my lips. The tension around us has yet to dissipate. The fact that Nick's Uncle is somewhere in this house is the only thing stopping us from ripping off each other's clothing and finishing what we started earlier on in the gym.

"I made the choice to be in your life. I will take whatever comes my way just so long as I can be with you, always and forever. I need you to be able to function... To live." I don't get the chance to answer him as he swiftly places his lips over mine. We can't be doing this so freely but I make no attempt to stop him. My phone buzzes in the back pocket of my shorts and my mind suddenly jolts to my earlier thoughts surrounding the text messages I was supposed to have received from my Mum. I turn my head to the side causing Nick to look at me in confusion.

"What's wrong?" Nick asks me with apprehension in his tone. I think he's becoming afraid to ask that question.

"Your Uncle said that Martha had text me just after the accident. I never received that text though. The only text I received was earlier this evening so unless it was delayed in coming through, I'm sure that isn't the one your Uncle is referring to. When you gave me the phone, had you already deleted those messages?" Nick looks wounded and looks down at his hands, instantly showing his guilt. I knew it.

"Why? Why did you do it? That's my phone, my messages... You had no right." I can't help the slight betrayal I feel. I'm sure Nick's reasons for doing so were justified but I just wish people would quit treating me as if I'm a toddler! I'm not as weak as I seem, I can handle things by myself.

"I'm sorry, I don't regret doing it. She had no right to message you so soon after everything happened. You needed some space and her message was basically pushing you to deal with all of this too soon. Like I said, I'm sorry but I don't regret it." I'm astounded at how brutally honest he is being. I appreciate it but it still stings.

"Thank you for your honesty. I'm going to go to bed. I need to message my Mum." With that, I give Nick a nudge to force him off of my lap. He reluctantly stands and allows me to move. Like a puppy nipping at my heels, he follows me closely as I make my way up the stairs. As I near my bedroom, I pick up my pace, enough so that it isn't obvious but enough that I'm ahead of Nick. As I reach my bedroom, I swiftly step inside and shut the door flicking the lock. Nick reaches my door just as the lock clicks into place. I feel awful for shutting him out but I want some alone time. I need to speak to my Mum and I know after that I'll just feel shittier than ever. I really hope Nick understands that.

Chapter 8, Nick:

She's shut me out again. I could've kicked myself over and over again when she asked about the text messages. I'm an idiot for thinking I could keep it from her. When did I become such a secretive person?

I'm dreading the outcome of this meeting tomorrow. It isn't my place to get involved, not really. Then again, I am involved. Much more involved than I wish to be. I've always been dragged into things I would rather not be. There was a time where Sam had been dating this girl. She was the complete opposite of him and to be honest, she was a bitch. She constantly put him down and made it her mission to lower his self esteem until he was left picking himself back up off of the floor. What started off as one night of listening to Sam moan about her, turned into every minute we were together. As his best friend, I listened and of course I cared. There is only so many times you can tell a person they are being destroyed until the day comes when their eyes open and they see the damaged pieces laying in front of them. I had held Sam in my arms the day his eyes had opened. He described feeling broken, like his heart had been violently ripped from his chest. The she devil couldn't have cared less. That's the thing with some relationships, one person can be the centre of your universe and you'll put all of yourself into that one person, but to them you are just a measly hill and once they've climbed you, they move on to their next challenge. I didn't mind being dragged into Sam's situation. I made sure I stayed in Sam's company as long as he needed me too. Sam is happy now. As much as I don't want to admit it, Sarah is the best thing that has ever happened to him. He conquered the devil and has been rewarded with his angel.

This situation is different. There is far too many people and emotions involved. Josie is my main priority but I cannot even begin to fathom how Uncle Sal feels. He and Martha are not only a couple, they're a whole unit. When I was taken in by my Uncle, he and Martha had only just begun dating. It makes sense now as to why I never met her face to face. She was hiding. Hiding from the unforgivable act she had committed. My Uncle is as forced into this conflict as I am... In a much worse way. Say he did know what Martha had done, how could you still see that person with such light and love? Surely witnessing the darkest parts of someone would be difficult to live with? How would I feel if Josie had a dark secret? Maybe she does...

I hear Josie's lock click and I jump away from the looming questions in my mind. Josie's face comes into view from around the door.

"I guess if you haven't got the hint by now, you won't at any point tonight. Come in." She turns her back to me, leaving the door open as an invitation. It is a bit creepy to be lurking outside of her door but truthfully, I felt lost. Rational Nick would have gone to his room but this whole night has knocked me for six.

Josie's bed is an explosion of photo albums, all opened at random points. The faces of men, women, adults and babies all look up through the shiny film holding them in place. In the middle of the sea of albums is an open notepad. Whilst waiting for me to come in, Josie retreated back to the bed and is now focused back on her task, pen in mouth. I watch her, trying to suss out her thought process.

"What are you doing?" She doesn't look up from her notebook as she prepares to answer me.

"I'm trying to see if there is anything obvious in any of these photographs that may give me some insight into my family. My Mum and Dad never really opened up about the subject. I know that my grandparents on my Dad's side of the family never liked my Mum but the reasons behind that were never disclosed. My Mum's parents were always lovely to me and my Mum, but they don't live here, they're both in New Zealand. We would go over to see them once a year but I haven't heard from them since my Mum was supposed to have died." The sadness of this admission radiates from her. I cannot help but feel some anger towards these two Grandparents that I don't know and doubt I will ever meet. They should have been there for Josie. They were supposed to have lost their Daughter. Maybe they had no inclination. I mean, Josie's Mum may well have kept in touch with them, they would never have suspected a thing.

Perching on the side of the bed, I peer at the open notebook. Josie has drawn a family tree with multiple different branches cascading all over the page. The opposite page is filled with questions and I know that Josie plans to really grill Martha when she sees her tomorrow. Can she be blamed? She deserves to know the answers to these questions. The girl is an adult now for Christ's sake. She isn't a petulant child anymore that needs wrapping up in bubble wrap. I know all too well that when you decide to keep things from someone, you are opening up a whole can of worms that can never be closed again. The worms become out of control, some of them can be crammed back into the can but there will always be some that get away. In a court setting, you are sworn to tell the truth, the whole truth and nothing but the truth, so why is this never applied to everyday life?

I blink rapidly to get myself out of my day dream state of mind. My eyes focus in on a photograph of four young adults, or possibly teenagers. I inch closer to it, just to make sure that my vision is not deceiving me, for there in front of me, is a younger version of my Uncle. Why would this particular photograph be in Josie's possession?

"Jos... Who are these people? That's my Uncle." I push my forefinger onto the picture I am referring to. Josie averts her gaze until we are both starting at the faces in front of us with the utmost intensity.

"That's my Mum and Dad... I have no idea why your Uncle is in the same shot with them. Maybe he knew them from school. My mum was only fifteen when this picture was taken..." Josie flips the image and scribbled words come into view. "Martha, Charles, Sal and Katrina... They did know each other then?" She directs the question at me like I'm supposed to have a fucking clue!

"My Uncle Sal told me that they met at work. That your Mum was a receptionist or something. I have no idea."

Josie frantically scribbles another question onto her page of ever-growing curiosities. When she sits up again, I nose at what she has written: 'how are you, Dad and Nick's Uncle connected?' This Katrina bird clearly means nothing to Josie and I also have no idea who she is, she doesn't look familiar. However, the question of how Josie's Mum, Dad and my Uncle have connections from that far back does need answering, and I know Josie well enough now to know that she won't let the matter slip from her mind.

"Nick... I'm terrified." I would be surprised if she wasn't, but hearing her say so with such emotion behind the words breaks my heart into two. As I turn my head to look at her, I see her eyes glazing over and her bottom lip trembling. It's indescribable as to how it feels to see my girl cry. If I could take away any harmful things or situations from this world, I would. Sadly, I know I can't protect her from everything. I look at her fixedly and pull her to my chest, relishing the feeling of her head burrowing into me. If she hadn't had littered the bed with those albums, I would lay us down so we are in a more comfortable position. Her hair is silky soft and smells like her usual apple scent. The scent that has become home to me.

"Josie, baby, sit up a moment. I'm going to move these off of the bed if that's okay so we can lay down?" Her head nods against me and I gently lift her up off of my body. Josie's eyes flick back and forth as she observes me folding up the collection of photographs and placing them delicately back onto the shelf. I motion my hand towards the lamp and stroll over to switch off the main light. As I turn back towards the bed, I can't help the audible gasp that escapes through my partially open lips. The orange light of the lamp hits Josie's face in the most angelic way. Her right cheek is illuminated by the soft lighting and her right eye twinkles. Her soft lips open ever so slightly as she realises how deeply I am staring at her. I feel like a whole year has passed before I can finally peel my eyes away from the woman sitting on the bed. If life meant eternity, I would never stop looking at her.

Josie moves over, making room for me as I slide into the bed, settling myself under the warm duvet. Like a monkey to its mother, Josie doesn't give me time to think before she has clung to my side, her leg thrown over my waist and her left arm draped across me also. She rests her head down on my chest and gently sighs. I know she's tired, and tomorrow will be beyond draining on her energy. I'm happy to be here in this massive bed, holding my love as she drifts off into the realm of sleep. As softly as I can manage, I kiss the top of her head, wishing her the kindest of dreams.

Chapter 9, Josie:

I have been awake for an absolute age. My heart hammers consistently against my bruised ribs and I cannot stop the waves of nausea that keep hitting me. Today is the day. I never saw this happening to me in a million years. I am sitting down with my should-be-dead Mother to discuss why she abandoned me to go and live her own life, all the while I was forced to live with the most unloving and uncaring Stepmother and Father. It sounds insane, right?! This is the sort of shit you see in movies. I have never really had the best of luck, but this feels like life is really fucking joking about with me. If there is a God, I imagine he is deliberately causing these crazy occurrences, and he is just creasing himself up as he watches me struggle my way through each of them.

Nick is still snoozing peacefully beside me, and I don't have the heart to wake him. I was supposed to message my Mum last night just before I decided to unlock my door and allow Nick to come in and keep me company. I just couldn't do it. I had no idea what to say to her. I typed out lengthy message after lengthy message but as quickly as I typed one, I would delete it again... The content of my messages made absolutely no sense at all and instead, sounded like the ramblings of a mad woman. Each message went along the same lines of *'how could you do this to me'* and *'you will never understand how hard I grieved for you, a woman whom I believed to be lost forever'*.

I inwardly pray that Nick's Uncle has arranged a time for Martha to come over, just so I do not have to do so. I hope she isn't expecting any displays of affection. I want nothing more than to throw my arms around her, to envelope her in the biggest and warmest hug, just like old times. I just can't. I have ached every day. Until you have a person to grieve, it is difficult to truly comprehend just how awful it feels to miss someone. There are times where you will imagine the day you are without a loved one, and you will feel a twinge in your chest. The real thing is so much fucking worse. Throw any idea of grief you have out of the window. I wouldn't wish a bereavement on my worst enemy. My Mum didn't die, but I still feel a loss. Whoever this woman now is, she is not the Mum I remember, and I doubt she will ever be the same again. Something caused her to run away, and I will be damned if she thinks she is leaving here today without a bloody good explanation.

As silent as a mouse, I raise myself to the side of the bed, giving myself a moment behind standing thanks to the complaints of my ribs.

Finally, my ribs stop their pulsating and the pain is tolerable. If I am going to get through today, I will be needing those painkillers.

I stop by the toilet to empty my bladder. Standing at the sink to wash my hands, I raise my eyes to the mirror positioned in front of me. The dark circles under my eyes have calmed down drastically and I am relieved that I no longer represent a Zombie. I decide to take the plunge and force myself to inspect the damage to my side. It has only been a couple of days, so I don't expect a dramatic recovery but the yellowing, bluey-grey that dons my skin like a tattoo still is a sight for my sore eyes, or any sore eyes for that matter.

Opening the bathroom door, I jump out of my skin as I nearly collide with a bare male torso. I know without having to look up that this is the torso of Nick's Uncle. I swear I've seen less hair on a bear.

"Oops, sorry love I should have waited. Are you okay?"

"Morning, no it's fine I was just coming out anyway. I'm okay, I slept probably the best I have in a few days. Are you okay this morning? Have you managed to speak to my Mum?" Poor Sal, it is so early to be bombarding him with so many questions. I cannot seem to help it; they are just pouring out. Possibly due to my embarrassment of walking face first into his bare chest.

"I'm chipper! Yes, I have, she'll be coming about lunchtime if that is okay?" Lunchtime, that's only two hours away!

"Umm, yeah… Yeah, no… That's absolutely fine by me. Lunchtime works." I hang my head and gracefully step aside, speed walking to the top of the stairs. I take the stairs as quickly as I can and head straight to the kitchen to make my essential morning cup of coffee. As I near the kitchen I hear movement. As I turn the corner, the most delicious sight catches my eye. Nick has his back to me as he pours hot water into two mugs. A tight, black T shirt clings to his muscular back and the only item of clothing on the bottom half of his body are a pair of shorts style boxers. I know I am in for a treat when he turns around to face me. I lick my lips as the image welcomes itself firmly in my mind.

My intrusive thoughts are interrupted as Nick finally comes to realise my presence. I wonder how couples contain themselves every day. I just want to jump his bones already. Nick holds out a steaming mug for me to go and collect. My eyes are on fire, burning into his with so much ferociousness. I focus my attention to the floor until I reach him.

"Good morning, beautiful. How are you this morning? Are you feeling ready for today?" I will always melt inside when he calls me names like that.

"Good morning," I smile at him flirtatiously. "I'm actually okay. I have you. If I have you, I will be fine. I promise." He combs his fingers through my hair and watches my face with pure adoration.

"Good, that is the answer I was hoping for. Now, let's go and take a shower."

***

My thumb taps atop my interlocked fingers. My palms are sweaty, and my legs will not stop moving. All signs of nervousness. Some-

With that, my Mum leaves her words hanging in the air as she stands and leaves the room. What is she talking about? Why would Nick need me for support? What are my Mum and Nick's Uncle keeping from the pair of us that is so terrible? Oh, good Lord, I hope Nick and I aren't related or something! I feel sick at the multitude of possibilities that swim through my thoughts. Why is nothing ever simple.

My Mum, Nick and Sal all walk into the room. All the blood appears to have drained from each of their faces. Nick sits beside me and grabs my hand. I welcome the warmness and safety I feel from his touch. His pupils are dilated, and he is chewing his bottom lip. I feel some sort of relief that he and I are as nervous as one another. I realise how ironic this is. Nick, myself, my Mum and Sal are basically mirroring one another in the way we are sat. Sal looks to my Mum and she looks back at him. One of them needs to speak first but I'm pretty sure one is waiting for the other to open their mouth. Nick clears his throat, shooting daggers towards the adults across from us.

"I'm sorry. My poor choices are the reason all of us are sitting here now. I should have been firmer and taken what I knew I wanted and needed many years ago now, the thing is it just wasn't as simple back then." My Mum speaks up first. She isn't wrong when she says this mess is because of her. No one else in the room, myself included, has spoken or made a noise. She seems to notice this and opens her mouth before closing it okay, almost like she's searching for the right words.

"Josie, me and your Father did love one another, I promise that. Some things are just never meant to be though... If I had known that I wouldn't go on to stay in love with him, that our love would have faded out, I would have cut that painful cord a long time ago."

"You didn't though, Mum. Dad found love with my Stepmother. He left you."

"I know, sweetheart. It's true that is the way it happened. It isn't the way it should have happened. I should have been the one to walk away." I can't help the hot tears that begin filling in my eyes. I promised myself this morning that no matter how painful the conversation became, I would not cry. To hear her say that she should have been the one to walk away, when she did anyway, cuts me down to my very core. Before I realise it, I'm laughing. It's more of a mocking laugh, full of spite rather than humour.

"Do you even realise how little sense you are making? You did walk away. Dad walked away first when he chose bitch face, and you walked away when you decided I wasn't enough!" I'm thankful for the way Nick places an arm around my waist. If it wasn't for him, I feel like I would've left the room already. The aim of this excruciating meeting is to get answers, by choosing to walk away I will have to accept that I will never get them. As I have said to myself numerous times now, I'll be damned if I leave this room without answers.

"You're right. You are absolutely right... In order for you to fully understand this I need to take you on a trip down memory lane. MY memory lane. I'll start right at the very beginning." She takes a deep, shuddery breath before pursing her lips together and looking up to the ceiling. Her hands are clasped together, almost like she's praying. Maybe she is. Maybe she feels that she needs the strength. Sal takes her hand in his and gives her a reassuring nod. She visibly melts into his eyes and I tear my gaze away from them both, I feel like I'm intruding on their intimate moment. My Mum looks back to me and smiles before continuing on with her explanation.

"So... Myself, Sal, your father and Katrina all attended the same Secondary School. We were a mixed bunch, the most unlikeliest of friends. Me and Katrina were best friends first and we had been since we were just toddling about. Katrina was dating Sal and Sal was best friends with your Dad. So of course, we all ended up as one big friendship group. Sal and Katrina were on and off for quite some time. One drunken night, when we were sixteen, all four of us had been at a house party. The lies I told your Grandparents so I could go", she chuckles to herself. Her eyes glowing as she relives the memory. "As always, Sal and Kat had got into one of their tiffs. Kat told me she was leaving and I didn't really get a chance to go with her. Well, one drink lead to many drinks and me and Sal here... Well we ended up doing the unthinkable. I betrayed Kat that day. My best friend. From that day on, I tried to stay as far from Sal as I possibly could. I started dating your Father, thinking that could keep my feelings for Sal at bay. Kat found out eventually but she forgave me, she was more pissed off at Sal and she was convinced that he had coerced me into it to get back at her. We left School but all of us kept in touch as we parted ways to different Colleges. Eventually, I left home and moved in with your Father. Kat and Sal kept on with their whole on and off charade. I got a job at a publishing company not too many years after leaving College. There was a charity event one evening and I nearly died from shock when the founder of the company was welcomed on stage. It's the cliché of 'the couple lock eyes from opposite sides of the room', but cliché or not, we were both transported back to a time full of intense feelings for one another. As you could have guessed, we both spent the night in one another's company. Your Father was back here at home, probably without a care in the world for his girlfriend who was over a hundred miles away. He's your Father so I will try to keep my feelings to myself, but he didn't really notice me unless there was a reason for me to be noticed; when he was able to gain something from my presence. Sal always made me feel like the only woman in the room. Well, this is where it gets really complicated..." My Mum leans across and whispers something unknown into Sal's ear. Whatever it was she said, he nods in agreement. In a fleeting moment, that if you blinked you would miss, I notice the look of unease in Sal's eyes. Whatever it is that my Mum is about to reveal will affect him to, in some way or another. He's a good man. He has raised Nick like his own Son. He gives to charity. I struggle to see the bad in him. I cross my fingers, hoping that whatever it is that I discover will not tarnish my view of him.

"After our evening together, I returned home. Kat phoned me later that evening and told me she was pregnant. I don't know why I bothered asking her at the time, but I had to be sure. I was right... Kat was pregnant with Sal's baby. I feigned happiness for her. I even went as far as to tell her that I would arrange her baby shower! When your Father spoke to me about the situation, I felt so sick that I had to leave the room. He kept calling us both 'Auntie and Uncle'. All I could see was my future with the man I loved being burnt to ash. There was no possible way that I could keep going back to Sal when he was about to have a baby. Anyway, a couple of months went by and I had these weird pains in my side accompanied by frequent vomiting. I went to my doctor and I actually laughed when he asked if I could be pregnant. I said no but to rule it out, the doctor sent me to the toilet so he could analyse a urine sample. The result came back positive. I had no idea how it was even possible, myself and Sal had been careful. That's the thing, nothing is impossible. To this day I still feel like it was nature's way of getting me back for hurting my best friend. I told your Father the same day I found out. I wanted to keep it a secret but it was eating me from the inside out. Your Father knew you wasn't his. We hadn't been intimate in such a long time. He handled it better than I expected... Until he found out who the Father of the life growing inside me was." I can't help the look of astonishment I am giving Sal. My Mum notices and halts her speech. My mind is in overdrive and, although I know what this must mean, I still feel the need to ask the question.

"So is Sal... Nick's UNCLE... My biological Dad?" I look sideways at Nick. He appears to be a mix of infuriation and nauseated.

"Yes Honey... That's exactly it."

"I'll be right back." I race from the room, the floor blurring underneath me as my legs take me away from the awkward, stale air of the room. I head to the bathroom and lock the door behind me, drawing in air at a rapid pace and allowing my mind to catch up. This is so fucked up. Once again, I've been screwed over. I allow myself to finally sob, as loudly as I need, into my knees that I have drawn up into my chest.

Chapter 10, Nick:

I feel sick to my stomach. I am rooted to the seat, my body still deciding whether to fight or flight. Josie made up her mind pretty quickly and do I blame her?! I wish I could run from this room but I know that my anger always leads me to doing stupid shit. Right now, I think my anger could take me to a level I never thought myself capable of. Before now, I was always certain that you should never hurt family. Now, I'm not so sure. I want to connect my fist with my Uncle's face, making fucking sure to leave an imprint of my fist in his skull. I'm scared that I wouldn't be able to stop if I got started and, even if she is to mostly blame for this mess, I hate starting violence in front of women.

I'm so worried about Josie, I can't imagine she's taking this lightly at all. Her Mum basically just confirmed that we are related. It would make us first Cousins. He knew back then as he knows now that Josie and myself are serious. He took matters into his own hands when he had no bloody right! My heated eyes meet his and he quickly looks down to the ground.

"So basically me and Josie are related? You've allowed us to enter into some sort of messed up, incestuous relationship and you made no attempts to stop it before it went too far? I really hope there's a good explanation for all of this." I'm amazed at how well I am keeping cool. It's more for Josie's sake than my own. The last thing I want is to freak her out further by screaming the walls down.

"I'm sorry lad. There is more to all of this of course. I would never have allowed you to carry on blindly if it were the case that you were related. The thing is... You aren't. I am your Uncle, Nick but

would be left in tatters and it could knock down everything he had worked so hard to build. So, the three of us agreed on that night, that you were not to know any of this until after your eighteenth birthday. You would then be old enough to make your own choices and have your own views on the matter."

"Okay. I understand that. So, Sal... Dad," I spit out harshly, "your reputation was more important than owning up to the fuckery you made? It takes two to tango." Sal is wounded. Tears are forming in his eyes. I'm being a complete bitch; I hear Nick gasp beside me as I deal the harsh blows to his Uncle. "Oh, one more question," I add, "if you're the Father to my Stepmother's kid, and you're also my biological Father... Doesn't that make Maxie my half sister?" I already know the answer to this but again, I need confirmation and clarity. I need it spelt out word by fucking word.

"Yes, that's correct, and Josie it really wasn't like that. Charlie was my best friend and I'd already hurt Kat so many times, I couldn't hurt anymore people. I knew you would have a better Dad than I could be to you. I loved your Mum to the point it hurt, but she wasn't mine. I had to let her go back then, for my own sanity and your Mum's." Bile rises in my throat; Sal clearly doesn't know that he couldn't have left me with a less uncaring man for a Father.

"You think you did the right thing, but believe me you did not. The man I grew up with was not Father material. My Stepmother hates me and my Father decided long ago that I just don't exist, there wasn't room for me in his life and now I understand why. It makes sense now as to why my Stepmother had so much hate for me. It makes sense that things she said to me over the years weren't aimed at me, they were aimed at you two. When she would tell me that I would turn out to be a 'whore like my Mother', she was referring to her best friend having sex and subsequently having a baby with the man she loved. Because of you, Mum, the man she loved never loved her back. He only had eyes for you and that must have killed her to know. I get it now... And I feel sorry for her. Years of anguish have been replaced with this massive burden of understanding. How do I deal with this shit? Not to sound childish but I didn't ask to be born. Because of your stupidity," I motion towards my Mum and Sal, "I was dragged into a love triangle of sorts that caused me years of abuse." Nick has moved his hand from mine to my thigh. I'm a wild inferno that Nick is desperately trying to throw buckets of water over. I've never been so mad in all my life, and I can feel Nick's unease at seeing me in this state. "I want to leave this room, but you still haven't explained the key part of all this... Why create an elaborate scheme that cost you so much? You must have had to do so much planning to ensure your secrets would never be uncovered. You must have had to look over your shoulder for such a long time. I cannot even imagine how anxious you must have felt. You could have just come clean and saved yourself all this hassle. So why didn't you?" Visibly shaking at this point, I hand the metaphorical microphone to my Mother, putting her directly in the spotlight.

"Because of money. It always comes down to money. Your Father's career has been plunging for years now and he needed some sort of security if it all fell apart. It is messed up, but he promised you a better life, if I had known he would have gone back on that promise, I would never have given in to his whims. I was a mess, Honey. I was sneaking around behind your Dad's back with his best friend. My own best friend, or so I thought, got her own revenge on me by luring your Father in. She doesn't love him; she is incapable of love as you have seen for yourself. I started to rely on alcohol... and a lot of it. Your Dad paid me a lot of money and explained that if I made myself scarce, he would fabricate a believable story. He had some friends in high places that would provide him the backup if it were needed. Why do you think there was never a news story? A car crash is always sure to make the local news, at least. Especially if that crash had resulted in a fatality. I did what your Father asked, so there was never any need for a story. Sal moved me in with him instantly and supported me through a massive bout of Depression. Like I said, leaving my

Daughter wasn't the easiest thing in the world to do... But at the time it was the right thing. I created a whole heap of shame when I had an affair. An even bigger heap when a child came out of that. This town is small, people talk as you already know. It would have made your life excruciating. You would have been known as 'the illegitimate child', and I could not have that happen to you because of something I did. I dreamt every day of your eighteenth birthday, practically dragging Sal out of the door the day it arrived. Your Dad contacted me that same day and, like a witch breaking a curse, made it clear that you were available now. I was able to be near you and speak to you without the fear of repercussions."

The room falls eerily quiet. The only sounds bouncing off the walls being those of four sets of breaths. Nick is set in stone beside me, his infuriation evidenced by the rapid rise and fall of his chest. All I can think is 'this all happened because of money and status'. Fuck my feelings. As long as the town was left in the dark about shit choices my Mother made. Since the last piece of the puzzle fell into place, a knot has been forming in my chest, slowly growing bigger and tighter. I feel like crying would be the release I need. Crying will unravel the aggravating knot inside of me, but all I can do is stare ahead. My eyes dead, along with any or all emotion I had started the day with.

Betrayal is far from what I feel. I feel like I was sacrificed.

I stand ever so gingerly and force my feet to take me away, away from the room where my own personal Judas resides. The Judas that betrayed me and watched as I was sacrificed over and over for the past few years.

I don't know where I'm headed but I let my feet take charge. I walk through the veil of darkness that is this house, and head down the driveway to freedom.

Chapter 12, Nick:

My eyes shoot lasers into the skull of Martha. So, the truth is out, but at what cost? She has broken Josie's heart into a million razor sharp pieces. She should be made to get down on her hands and knees among the shattered pieces, her hands made to tear as she attempts to piece the shards of her Daughter's heart back together. Instead, Martha is just sat like stone, staring off into the distance as my Uncle grazes his thumb back and forth across her knuckles. Telepathically, I urge him to man up and look me in the eye, but I know he won't.

Josie ran off and I don't blame her, I would have done the exact same thing. I have so much admiration for that girl, to hear something like that and to just take off. I feel like I'd have done so much worse. They used her. The girl didn't ask to be born amongst all of this fuckery or deceit, and they just used her for their own gain. They fail to see how bright she shines, how she radiates and takes over a room. Souls such as Josie's do not exist anymore. She is rare.

With a sigh, designed to announce my annoyance and departure from the room, I raise myself and stalk out. A gust of wind slaps me in the face and I walk towards the source of said coolness to find the front door swinging gently. I have no idea where Josie has disappeared to, but I know for sure I need to start my search away from this house.

"Please just call me. I need to know you're okay." This is the second voicemail I have left for Josie in under five minutes. I really just need to hear her say she's somewhere safe. After the whole car crash fiasco, I would rather die than have to go through that torment again. My phone buzzing fills me with hope until I glance at the screen to see my Uncle's name illuminating back at me. My eyes involuntarily roll up into my head. How has he not taken the hint yet? Normally, after the first couple of attempts, people tend to lay off and decide to try again later. Not my Uncle though, he's just being incessantly annoying! Maybe I need to make the message clearer... I hit the angry, red button on the screen and shove my phone down deep into the back pocket of my jeans, a habit I still haven't managed to curb.

I make it into town, a row of pale bricked buildings with hanging colourful signs greeting me. I take a moment just to survey the hustle and bustle of people in front of me, looking out for my ray of light. Of course, I don't spot her.

I grit my teeth and make my way to the first Café. The problem with this small but quaint town is the sheer number of Cafés and restaurants. I guess I'll just have to do some trial and error.

Chapter 13, Josie:

I made it into the Town Centre. With no inclination of where I am heading, I just decide to walk until somewhere takes my fancy. The angry ball in my stomach has started to unravel ever so slightly, dissipating at the speed of a snail.

A dimly lit neon sign catches my eye. *'Mario's'*. A bar. This is exactly what I need. I steal a glance inside my bag, and I am relieved to find my purse is nestled at the bottom amongst all the other shit I need to sort through. I'm quite lucky to look so mature for my age. I've only been in a bar one other time in my life and I was underage. I remember the dismay on my Stepmother's face as I stumbled back through the door plastered at six in the evening. God, I wish I wasn't such a lightweight! I called my Stepmother a bitch that night. I felt the sting from her slap for about a week following that... It was brilliant though. I realise I am chuckling to myself at the memory, earning a few odd looks from strangers passing by.

I swing the door open to *'Mario's'* and step into the rustic style bar. From the outside, one could be fooled on the size of the place. *'Mario's'* is filled with the most beautiful artwork. I find myself drawn to a black and white print of a stag, the magnificent creature staring directly back at me. I find myself directly in front of the print, my hand brushing lightly over the dried paint. This artist must have really spent some time and effort on this piece.

"Josie?" I jump and snap my head up to the masculine voice addressing me. I find myself looking into warm hazel eyes, hiding behind black framed glasses. Simon. Does he have a fucking death wish?

I begin to stalk away when a hand on my elbow halts me in my tracks. I whip around, ready to release hell fire when I notice how sombre Simon looks. I know that look all too well. It's a look full of regret and worry. His eyes keep flicking to look around us, clearly searching to make sure Nick is not lurking nearby.

"Josie... I can't even begin to tell you how sorry I am for that night. I'm not that type of person at all and the fact that I even tried to pull that shit has eaten me up since I did it... Nick was right to beat the shit out of me. Even if it was agonising and I had to carry around a black eye for a while," Simon laughs and diverts his gaze to the ground out of embarrassment, I guess. "I haven't touched a drop of alcohol since that night and I doubt I ever will again. You have every right to tell me to fuck off, but it would put my mind at peace, and would mean the world to me, if you accept my apology." Simon extends his hand out to me. Sighing, I grip it and he visibly relaxes. I've never been one to hold grudges and, after Nick's assault, I doubt he'll be attempting to pull that shit again any time soon.

"Thank you for being man enough to do that face to face. The past is the past. You seem cool. I know you said you wouldn't touch alcohol again, but I am in desperate need of a drink after the day I've had. Care to join me? Of course, you can have a Cola or whatever." Simon's face lights up and he begins nodding, stroking the stubble on his chin as he does so.

"That would be great. I'll buy the first round; I owe that to you. You can tell me all about your crap day. What's your poison?" We walk over to the bar together. The air around us is still a little awkward as we attempt to figure one another out. I know his apology is sincere, but it still doesn't change what happened. This is the first time I've seen him since the whole charade occurred so awkwardness can only be expected, I suppose.

The barmaid, a petite lady with flame red hair and colourful tattoos spilling from her tank top stands before us, ready to take our order. I put in my order of a Cuban, earning a raised brow from

Simon. I give him a sideways smile and a small shrug. He obviously didn't peg me as a spirits girl.

A shrill chime erupts from within my bag. I know it's pointless looking at the screen, Nick has tried calling me since I left the house and each time, I've waited for it to ring off. This time, I decide to reassure him I'm okay. I raise my hand to Simon and gesture to the door. Simon nods back at me and signals that he'll be waiting.

Stepping outside, I dig my phone from the small pocket in my bag and swipe up to answer.

"WHAT. THE. HELL. I have been going out of my mind! Where are you? Are you okay? It's so selfish of you to go off like that. Do you not remember being hit by a car?" I take the phone away from my ear, his booming voice causing my eardrums to vibrate. Maybe I have been a little selfish...

"Hey, calm down... I'm okay. I just needed some time out. I'm just having a drink with an old friend and I'll be home. Wait for me there. I promise, nothing bad will happen." When in the history of all words has 'calm down' been effective? Great one Josie, I'll just have added fuel to the fire for sure.

"CALM DOWN! Please tell me that's a joke... Why is it so hard for you to accept that there are people who worry about you? Who's this friend? Is it Sarah?" Here we go...

"I'm okay. Please believe me. You would have wanted some time and space if you were in this situation. I bumped into Simon... Simon from the party... The one you beat to a pulp..." The silence on the other end of the phone is absolutely deafening.

"Where are you?" Okay, not as bad as I anticipated...

"Don't worry. I don't want you to come and make a scene. Simon is pretty scared of you, I'm not sure you being here will do much to calm his nerves."

"Since when did that creep's feelings matter more than your Boyfriend's? Josie, where are you?" We are going around in circles.

"Nick, just go home and wait for me. I shouldn't be anymore than an hour. I love you." I hang up and quickly power off my phone, shoving it deep into the abyss of my bag. My heart hammers again my ribcage, causing little shocks as a result. I take some long, deep breaths.

Stepping back into the bar, I head over to Simon. He looks at me quizzingly as I perch on the barstool beside him. I raise my glass of deep brown liquid, nodding my head as a way of saying thanks as I take the biggest mouthful, welcoming the sharpness of the Rum as it hits my taste buds.

"You look like you needed that. So, Josie Martin, what brings you here?"

~

What feels like an eternity later, I have bought Simon up to speed with the crazy happenings in my life. He listened intently as I started with meeting Nick, all the way to the past couple of hours. I could have sworn his eyes were ready to pop out of his skull when I mentioned my Mother faking her own death.

"Jesus, girl! How have you not gone absolutely insane?" Good question, Simon. Good question indeed. I feel as if I should be off the rails by now, but for some reason I have this overwhelming sense of calm about me... Maybe now I can begin to focus on the positives in life and move on to bigger and better things. I just can't shake the feeling that the worst is yet to come. It's terrifying to feel so calm and yet feel so terrified. It's a battle between heart and mind.

I really needed this. I needed to be able to rant about everything that has happened and to be able to laugh about it. Nick is too serious with this stuff. If I laugh, he frowns. Simon laughed along with me as we sipped our drinks. True to his word, Simon has stuck with non-alcoholic beverages.

One drink turned into two, which turned into three. If Simon hadn't of pulled that little stunt of his on the night of Nick's party,

I feel that we would have been friends from the get go. I shuffle slightly on the stool and awaken my bladder.

"I'm just paying a visit to the little girl's room, won't be a tick." I rise from the stool, wobbling slightly as I stand. Shit... Maybe three drinks were a bit much for Ms. Lightweight over here.

The Women's toilets are pristine and follow the Rustic theme of the Bar. There's a slight floral fragrance in the air and I welcome the scent as it fully hits my nostrils. I make it to a cubicle and gently close the door. Fuck, Nick is going to be so pissed off with me. Maybe I was a tad theatrical with cutting him off, followed by switching my phone off completely. As much as I love the person Nick is, he can be completely infuriating with his over protectiveness. More than likely this is due to being forced to fend for myself since the dawn of time, I guess I'm just used to being my own protector.

I pull the chain and leave the stall, making my way to the basins to wash my hands. I catch a glimpse of my reflection in the mirror: hair unkempt and a slight flush to my cheeks as a result of the booze. Besides that, I look refreshed. I don't feel as if I have that whole 'zombie vibe' about me anymore.

It's definitely time to head home.

Leaving the Women's toilets, I round the corner and nearly die on the spot as a Nick shaped figure sits on the stool I was sitting at, his stone-cold eyes meeting mine. His gaze is so intense, but I stand my ground. I didn't do anything wrong by having a drink with a friend, but I'm prepared to receive a grilling nonetheless. Simon may have his back to me but I can tell by his rigid posture that he feels intimidated. I hope Nick has played nice!

Simon turns to look at me as I reach the two Men. He chooses not to meet my eyes as he hands me my bag. Before I have the chance to take it from him, Nick's hand whooshes between us as quick as a flash and my bag ends up in his grip. I look at him in horror, mortified at his behaviour. Simon stands.

quivering mess.

"Come here," he grabs my waist and pulls me to him, my breath hitching in my throat at the sudden force.

"Oh shit, your ribs. Josie I'm so sorry. Did I hurt you?" I love this Man.

"Not at all, quite the opposite. You have no idea how you affect me," I bite my own lip as I say these words. They're nothing but the truth.

"Oh Baby, you have no idea how YOU affect ME."

We stumble through the mess that is Nick's bedroom until we reach his bed.

We spend the next hour finishing what we started in the Gym. As my final orgasm rolls over me, I tell Nick I love him. He finds his own release and comes to a halt above me. Rolling off of me, he lays behind me and pulls me to him, my back flush against his chest.

"I love you, Josie. Please never leave me. You own me, body and soul." We both drift off in each other's embrace, those words floating around my head and embedding in my dreams.

Chapter 14, Nick:

Still on a high from last night, I woke at seven just as daylight had begun to break through my curtains, and got to work on my monstrosity of a bedroom. I decided to keep the whole 'I trashed my bedroom when you wouldn't let me in to see you' story from Josie. The last thing I wanted to do was to make her upset. It isn't her fault that my temper comes from my Father. Although, unlike my Father, I'm not a waste of space drunkard that takes his anger out on his wife or kid.

Carefully manoeuvring the room so as not to wake Josie, I make a start on the Mount. Everest of clothing. A small sigh hits my ears and I glance up at the bed just in time to catch Josie smile as she dreams. Oh, my sweet girl, you deserve all the best dreams and more.

I finally put my Uncle out of his misery by sending him a quick text shortly after I got out of bed. I thanked him for encouraging Martha to tell Josie the full story and I asked that he ensure Martha gives Josie the space she needs to process everything. My Uncle is a good man but I can't get it out of my head that he isn't biologically my Uncle. The Man has moved Heaven and Earth for me, knowing that I'm technically not his Nephew. Maybe it isn't as true as they say it is: maybe, just maybe, water can be a little bit thicker than blood. I mean, my Father just abandoned his own Son like it was nothing, clearly blood meant nothing to him.

I glance up at my girl as she peacefully slumbers. I search her face from a distance, looking for signs that she is truly my Uncle's Daughter. There isn't even a hint. All I see is a youthful Martha reflected in her face.

How did my Uncle go on for so long knowing that he had another child; a beautiful girl with the world behind her eyes and her heart on her sleeve. It must have killed him to be in a room with her sometimes and to have to watch on as she called another man 'Dad'. I know for sure it would eat me up completely.

Satisfied that I have separated my clothing correctly: dirty stuff in one heap and clean clothes folded nearly in a stack, I make my way to my wardrobe and begin putting the clean clothes away as neatly as I can manage.

I wonder how Josie's Stepmother will feel knowing that the truth is out. Everything has fallen into place, and I know Josie feels sympathetic towards the Woman. It still isn't a bloody excuse though! Josie was merely a pawn in this whole thing, she didn't deserve to be treated so horridly over something she couldn't control. I want to feel sympathy for the Woman, I really do... But I just can't help but feel more bitterness towards her. Josie's Step-mother dragged innocent people into her revenge scheme, and look how that worked out. It'll probably anger her to no end. That Woman seems to love having control over everything she can; I doubt she saw this coming. She's been sussed.

"Good morning, I can't believe my eyes, I must still be dreaming." I whip around towards the voice of my angel. I love her this way: hair tousled from sleep and a languorous expression stretched across her perfect face. This is how I'll always love her.

"Don't make me stop what I'm doing and come over there," I threaten, hoping I can actually go over there. In response to my light-hearted threat, she throws back the duvet to reveal her temple of a body. Open and ready for me... All mine. I make no hesitation of pushing myself from my sitting position on the floor and stalking towards her, as if she is my prey and I the predator. She licks her lips in anticipation as I remove my shirt and boxers before crawling my way up the bed. I nestle between her thighs and she raises her legs, crossing her ankles over my lower back. I'll always want this. I'll always want her.

Chapter 15, Josie:

"Okay great, I'll see you tomorrow." I hang up, ending my conversation with Sarah. I decided tomorrow I'll go back to college, back to a part of my life that offered some kind of normality.

My ribs are still visibly bruised and over exertion causes them to complain, but other than that I'm ready to go back. I've already lost so much time.

I'm about to place my phone down on the dresser when it chimes again. The screen lights as I raise it up to my line of vision, Maxie's name coming into view. I swallow the lump in my throat. I still haven't spoke to her properly since finding out that we're actually related. Half-sisters. I've always loved Max like a sister, but now I can say that she IS my sister. My heart goes mad when I think about the conversation I'll need to have with my Stepmother. I can't actually think of a time where we've managed to sit in the same room and converse without some type of nasty comment being thrown.

'Hey, where have you been? We need to catch up whenever you're free'. I feel so guilty for abandoning her, because that's basically what I've done.

'Hi, I'm so sorry life has just been crazy! Are you free tomorrow afternoon? I have college in the morning'. I'll have to tell her tomorrow. There's no plausible way I can be within a two-metre distance of Max and not tell her. She'll either hug me or hit me. We have never kept secrets from one another, ever.

Nick appears in the doorway, his wet hair in a tangled mess on top of his head. A few strands have broken loose and hang down over his forehead. The only dignity he allows himself is the towel covering the bottom half of his body. There's a weird silence between us that I can't figure out. This morning was magical in every way. He worshipped my body until I was a mess, calling out his name as I fell apart around him. So, I'm not able to understand why we're both so far from one another, neither one of us speaking.

Just as I'm about to let the silence completely take over, Nick speaks.

"Do you really have to go back tomorrow? Surely you can't feel ready to face the real world already?" Nick's peeks out from under his lashes at me in the most solemn of ways.

I need to move forward and carry on with life. I can't stay cooped up in my own bubble for much longer, otherwise I may just go slightly stir crazy. I still have hopes and ambitions; I want to be successful.

"I'll be fine. Sarah will be there and she's promised to meet me at the gate so we can walk in together. Do you really think Sarah will let me crumble? That girl is made of strong stuff, she radiates 'strength'," I cock one eyebrow, daring Nick to disagree with my statement on Sarah. He doesn't, he just begins to lightly chuckle. The tension in the room leaves us alone.

"Okay, fine. Promise me you'll text as soon as you get there, and as soon as you reach your first class. Hell, text me whenever you can!"

"We still have all of today before I actually go back! You're speaking as if I'll be leaving in the next hour." I'm still adapting to the whole 'someone caring about me to the point that I'm on their mind all day, everyday' thing. I feel that Nick is being irrational, but no one has ever cared about me, or my life this deeply. I am so used to going unnoticed. I felt like I could walk into a room of people, scream my lungs to pieces and still no one would bat an eyelid at me. I take a few steps towards my Boyfriend and circle my arms around his waist, hugging him flush to me. I hear a small breath leave him as I squeeze him tight. He smells fresh from his shower and his chest still slightly damp. The feeling I liken to that of Heaven. I'm so blessed.

~

I fling my bag over my shoulder and place my hand in Nick's. This is it... Back to the real world. I'd be lying if I said I wasn't a tad nervous about today. It's in people's nature to be nosey, and I'm sure my presence, or lack of, would have been discussed at some point. Not because anyone truly cares, but because people thrive off gossip. Hopefully Sarah will have told them all to shut the fuck up.

Nick has been tense all morning, from the moment we both woke to now, he hasn't said very much. I know he thinks this is a bad idea. He's had me all to himself for the past few days and he is reluctant to share me with a college full of people, I get that because I feel exactly the same with him. Either way, our education cannot wait much longer and if I don't make it to University at the end of the year, I'll forever kick myself. I've had many regrets in my short time on this earth. Life is so short and the Grim Reaper waits for no soul. When your time is up, it's up. No second chances. The thought of this used to send me in a massive panic attack, but now I welcome the thought, it pushes me to strive for great things. I want to go out of this world with absolutely no regrets.

We reach the college with plenty of time spare. I send a quick message to Sarah to let her know I'm here and waiting before turning to face Nick. A muscle noticeably ticks in his jaw, evidence that something has him wound up.

"Are you okay? Today will be fine, I promise."

"It isn't the college thing that I'm worried about... It's later, when you go to see Maxie. What happens if your Stepmother is there? Will you tell her that you know?" Shit. The thought had fleeted across my mind momentarily after I had texted Max, but I hadn't thought any deeper into it since then.

believe soul mates can be anybody. They can be your best friend, your parent or in my case, your Sister. A soul mate is someone who knows you inside and out. They know your deepest secret and they know what makes your heart skip a beat. They pick you up when you fall and make time for you, even if they have a hectic life. They have looked deep into your eyes, the windows to the soul, and witnessed first-hand what your soul looks like. They know what makes you, you... Period. Maxie is my soul mate, my soul Sister. God, have I missed her!

We both calm down enough to pull away from one another so we can have a proper greeting. I finally get a proper look at her. She is... Glowing. There's something very different about her. She's oozing confidence and her smile seems to have grown even more radiant than I remembered.

Max takes me by my forearm and leads me up the stairs. When we're in her room, the room we used to call ours, I finally feel safe. The pressure on my chest slowly eases.

Max wrings her hands. She's nervous about something. Oh Jesus, I have a feeling there'll be two big revelations dropped today. The question is: who goes first?

"Max, I have something to tell you..." Maxie begins to laugh nervously.

"I actually have something to tell you as well... Do you want to go first?"

"My something is quite complicated, so it's best that you go first," we're both as anxious as the other. That's something, I guess...

Maxie doesn't say anything, instead she places a hand on her stomach and splays her fingers. No... My eyes widen in surprise, hoping that her actions are what I think they are; that what she's trying to tell me is what I think it is.

"Max, what's going on?" I can't help the smile in my voice. Some happy news is so needed it's almost unreal.

"You're going to be an Auntie. Me and James are expecting! I'm twelve weeks. Believe me, I was so shocked when I found out! I'd been so unwell for days but I never expected it to be pregnancy! Once myself and James got over the petrifying prospect of being parents, we quickly became excited. I'm going to be a Mumma! How amazing is that?!" Maxie's voice gradually went up octaves as she revealed the news. I'm so thrilled for her. She'll be the most amazing Mum. Like the sap I am, I start crying. This time it's tears of joy.

"Fucking hell! Max, that's amazing! I'm so happy for you! Come here," I pull to me, encasing her in my arms as tight as I can.

"Thank you! Just a pre-warning, you'll be on babysitting duties when me and James need a break," she laughs but I would happily do it! I'm going to have a Niece or Nephew, how exciting?!

"Happily! Sign me up for ALL of the babysitting duties!" I exclaim "Where are you guys going to live? Have you discussed that yet?"

"We have. I'll be moving in with James. His place is so much bigger and there's the added bonus that his place is his. No parents to worry about." Max winks at me, obviously referring to the Stepmonster. I'm shocked that Max didn't move in with James sooner. They're always together as it is. I get it though, being young and all.

"Ah, got ya. Well, I'll be with you every step of the way. I'm sorry I've been a crappy Sister lately. So much has happened... Sister of mine." I add emphasis on the 'Sister' and Max just looks at me without a clue as to what I'm doing.

"Okayyy... Why are you speaking weirdly?" It's now or never.

"You're my Sister... Well, my half Sister but to say that just sounds ridiculous." Max's eyes widen as she slowly processes what I'm saying and what it means. Her mouth parts and she looks at me vacantly. I've dug a hole now and there's no going back.

I spill my guts to her and she sits patiently, listening intently to each and every word.

When I have uttered the last revelation, I stop and wait for her to say something. Max just stares at the floor, tears welling up her eyes, threatening to spill. I can't read her.

"I don't understand... Why didn't Mum tell me? Why am I always the last to find out things? This is huge. So, Charlie isn't your Dad?"

"Nope... Doesn't it all make sense now though? Your Mum despises me because my own Mum fucked her over, basically. My Mum had the heart of the man your Mum loved. They were best friends for goodness' sake! I can't imagine hurting my best friend like that. It must have been awful. I can only image the depth of the betrayal and how it would sting. In a way, I feel so sorry for your Mum. It doesn't give her an excuse to make the past few years of my life hell, but I get it." Max lets out a sigh and shuffles over to me, resting her head on my shoulder.

Minutes tick by and we sit like this, neither one of us making an effort to move. My head hurts with the intensity of everything that has taken place so far this afternoon.

A knock on the door brings us back to reality with a harsh slap.

"Maxie, Honey. I'm home. Can I come in?" My Stepmother. Shit.

"Does she know I'm here?" I whisper to Max. She shakes her head.

"Hey Mum, you can but Josie's here." There's a pause outside the door before my Stepmother's shrill tone returns.

"Oh... Well, I'll be downstairs." We hear her feet descend on the stairs and I let out the breath I didn't even realise I was holding.

"I need to go and speak to her. I need her to know that I know. I'd be foolish to think it'll change anything, but miracles can happen. Do you want to come?" I need to address my Stepmother sooner or later. I'm being a coward just hiding out up here with Max.

"Oh, I'm coming! I know my Mother; she likes to twist things. As much as I love her, I'll always back you if I know she's wrong." I smile at Max. She's too good to me. If it hadn't been for her, these few years would have been unbearable.

Shaking, I open the bedroom door and make my way down the

stairs with Max in tow.

I head to the lounge, the sound of the television giving away that my Stepmother is there. As I enter the room, she looks up at me with her dark, pointy eyes. Sometimes I feel she's Medusa. I always used to avoid her gaze, it's harsh enough to turn anyone to stone. Standing here now, I have no choice but to look at her. For once I need to stand tall and show that I am capable of not being a push over.

Max makes her way to the sofa and beckons for me to join her in the spare seat beside her. Gingerly, I creep my way over to her and sit down as gently as I can. Fucking hell, could this be anymore awkward? My Stepmother clicks her tongue in annoyance. Looks like I have to be the first to speak.

"I know... I know about you, my Mum and Sal. I know that Sal is my Dad. I'm sorry for the way you were treated, it was unfair." For the first time ever, I spot a flash of emotion make its way across my Stepmother's usually composed face. It's only a fleeting moment of emotion, but I'll take it. Her hurt and shock is quickly replaced with anger. Her fists clench and I notice her jaw become tight as she grits her teeth. My heart begins to thump erratically and I put myself on edge, ready to fight or flight.

"Get. Out. Now." My Stepmother spits venom in my direction and stands sharply, throwing her arm out and gesturing at the door. I stand from my seat and suddenly I'm thrown back to three years ago...

Three years ago:

'" Why would your Dad ever love you? You're just a spoilt little brat who loves getting her own way. Why did you tell your Dad you love him? Do you really think he loves you back? You're a nuisance in his life. If only your selfish Mother hadn't gone and got herself killed, we wouldn't be lumbered with a little rat like you. Just go, get out of my sight! You make me feel sick! "

I begin to make my way from the room, tears streaming down my face *and shame tugging at my heart. Was it wrong to tell my Dad I love him? I don't tell him often enough... There's no emotion between us. I just wanted to hear my Dad tell me he loves me too. Instead, he tattled on me, laughing right into my face as soon as I said those four fatal words: 'I love you Dad'... Something ordinary that pretty much every child tells their parent. If only my situation were normal.*

'smack'

Pain radiates through the right side of my face as my Stepmother's hand collides with my cheek. I knew it was coming but that doesn't mean it hurts any less.

Present:

Maxie remains seated on the sofa in utter shock. She stares at my Stepmother like she's the devil reincarnate.

Just as I make my way from the room, my Dad appears and my composure slowly crumbles that little bit more. I bite the inside of my cheek to keep from bawling, any sign of weakness is a disadvantage. I learnt that from very early on. My Dad looks shocked to see me standing in front of him. He looks between me and my Stepmother, attempting to gauge the atmosphere in the room. My Stepmother rushes to his side and whispers something in his ear. Whatever she said visibly ignites his rage. When my Dad gets mad, the first noticeable sign is the deep purple that creeps up his neck before taking over his whole face.

"LEAVE! I THOUGHT WE HAD MANAGED TO ESCAPE THIS MESS!" My Dad's voice booms, ricocheting from every wall in the room. In my peripheral vision, I see Maxie flinch, her hand flying to her stomach. A new found confidence within me ignites and I clench my fists, locking my eyes onto my Dad's, ready to lay all the cards on the fucking table.

"Well, 'Dad'.... Ha! Thank fuck you don't really get the honour of holding that title. There are many couples out there who are desperate for kids. People who deserve to have Children but just simply cannot. You had the chance to be a Dad, but you failed. You'll die alone and angry with a woman who is only with you out of revenge. Look at you, you look like an angry, purple, tiny man. You're a mess! You chose not to tell me; I was bound to find out sooner rather than later. Now quit your yelling, you're stressing Max out!" I don't even give him a chance to answer as I storm past him, shoving him hard as I make my exit. It felt so good to get all of that out in the open.

I slam the front door behind me, not caring if it pisses my Stepmother or Dad off. I vow never to step foot in that formidable house again. For all I care, it can burn to the ground and take the demons that inhabit it back to the gates of hell they came from.

Nick comes into view from around the corner as I step away from the house. I gawp at him, feigning shock that he didn't stay away as he promised. I'm grateful.

I run straight into his arms and immediately feel at home. The anxious ball that had formed over the duration of my visit finally unravels in the most embarrassing way as I collapse into fits of laughter.

Nick holds me at arm's length, intrigued by my reaction and desperately waiting for me to give him the lowdown on what happened. His cocked eyebrows only make the situation funnier. Finally, the bubbles in my stomach die down and I'm able to speak.

"You will not believe the fucking afternoon I've had. Come on, let's go home and I'll tell you everything."

Chapter 16, Nick:

Mind blown... That's all I can say. That's all I feel. We arrived home and I wasted no time in sitting us down for Josie to spill the beans. On the drive home, she was practically shaking with excitement to tell me everything. My Girl never fails to surprise me... I'm so damn proud of her for standing up to those monsters! As for Maxie... I have no words. Maxie will be an amazing Mother, unlike her own Mother.

I had spent the duration of Josie's visit standing on the corner of the street. I plugged in my headphones to take my thoughts away from the endless possibilities that could have been occurring behind the closed door. A few strangers had passed and given me weird looks. I must have looked odd just standing on the corner of the street with my hands in my pockets and my head bobbing along to the music blaring into my ears. I couldn't have given two shits how it looked, I wanted to be there in case my Girl needed me. Fuck going home and being too far away. With the type of people her Stepmother and Father are, anything is possible.

My head had swum with dark thoughts of potential situations. The thought of them hurting Josie had nearly been enough to send me hammering on the door, but I quickly remembered my promise and remained firmly where I stood.

I thought it odd that Josie's Stepmother and Father had reacted the way they had when the news broke. I mean, if it were me in their shoes, I would be glad that I no longer had to keep such a big secret.

My thoughts are interrupted by Josie as she calls me to dinner. I rise and head to the kitchen area. On the bar sit two steaming plates of the most mouth-watering looking food. From the smell, it looks as if she has cooked some sort of Chicken Pasta. The smell is just divine. My stomach rumbles in agreement.

We sit in silence, both of us demolishing our plates as if we've been starved. I let out a few audible moans as I eat, earning a proud smile from Josie. God knows where she learnt to cook, but I'm grateful to wherever or whomever it was.

When we finish our meal, I gather our plates and cutlery and proceed to tidy up. She cooked so I'll clean, that's only fair. When I was younger, I watched my Mum constantly scurry around after my Dad. She was basically his Mother as well as his Wife. I always vowed never to be like that. Women do not become our significant others to rush around after us. There are some Men out there that give the rest of us Men bad names, my Father being one of them.

Josie watches me as I finish the last of the tidying, her elbow rests of the Island in the middle of the Kitchen and her head rests in her palm. She gives me a wink and sashays out of the Kitchen, putting on a show. I love watching her walk away from me. Her hips swaying seductively and her backside prominent in her tight jeans. Fuck it, the rest of this can wait until tomorrow.

I creep after her, but she's already disappeared up the stairs. Taking the stairs two at a time, it doesn't take me long to reach her bedroom, where I find her removing her shirt. I stand in the doorway and watch. She is aware of my presence and carries on stripping, continuing her show. It takes all my self-control not to storm over to her and remove the remainder of her clothing for her, especially when she bends to untie her boot laces. She doesn't realise just how enticing she is. Josie is the full package. A heart of gold and the most desirable body. I remember the way she rushed to cover herself during our first time together, an action which annoyed me to no end.

Josie turns to face me and my face lights up like a kid at Christmas. Her matching underwear is enough to drive me wild. She wears a matching cream coloured lacey bra and Brazilian style underwear. I've never seen this set before... I'm rendered speechless.

She walks over to me as if she is a model on a catwalk.

She stands in front of me and begins to trail her finger over my chest, forming small circles as she bites her bottom lip.

"Jesus Woman, please stop biting your bottom lip or you'll be the death of me."

"Oh yeah, make me." Game on.

Josie darts around me preparing to run, but I'm too worked up for a game of Cat and Mouse. Using lightening reflexes, I grab her around the waist. She squeals in my arms and flails about. I spin her and throw her over my shoulder, slapping her arse playfully. She giggles as I carry her to the bed and fling her down. I begin to hastily remove my own clothing, listening to Josie as she mewls in anticipation. She has no idea what is in store for her...

~

I run my fingers through the shiny, blonde hair that splays over my chest. Both spent from our passionate love making. Josie is oddly quiet.

I tilt my head to the side and remove my hand from her hair to place my fingers under her chin. She looks up at me, her eyes duller than usual. Shit, did I do something?

"Hey, what's going on?" I ask her.

"Nothing much. I'm just thinking of how my Stepmother reacted to me. I said that I was sorry. I apologised for my own Mum's behaviour and it's like she didn't even hear it. She was just so blinded with rage at the fact that I now know everything. It's almost as if she enjoyed this whole secretive thing and would rather I was still in the dark, why do you think that is?" I'm relieved I'm not the only one who finds that Woman's reaction weird, but to see how it's affecting Josie tugs on my heart strings.

"I know Baby, you didn't do anything wrong. I have no idea why she reacted that way, maybe she's just so used to being angry at everything and anything so now it's an automatic reaction. Try not to think about her. She isn't worth any of your brain power." Josie sighs and gives me a half-hearted smile before resting her head back on my chest.

After a couple of minutes of silence, I look down at her to find her eyes closed and her mouth parted. She's had a long day and I'm amazed she's lasted this long being awake.

I can't help the hatred I feel towards her Stepmother. Josie has so much love to give, her heart so large. Besides that wretched Woman, there is not another person on this earth that dislikes Josie, so that says a lot. I understand why she feels angry at the situation, but Josie didn't cause it. Josie was merely a factor in the events that unfolded all that time ago. Her Stepmother ended up hurt because the Man she loved, loved her best friend instead. She had the chance to become a strong Woman and use her anger towards them in a positive way, but instead she chose to make a young Girl's life a living nightmare. A young Girl who thought she had lost her Mum... That's the thing about people who choose to abuse others, they are the weakest of the weak. They are so full of negativity and darkness that they feel it's a need to inflict suffering to feel something. They do not care of the repercussions or how they may end up ruining a life. In their eyes, ruining someone's life is an achievement. They see no wrongdoing on their part... Abusers are the true demons of the Earth.

~

Day two of College is far easier to deal with, possibly because I know Josie isn't going on some suicide mission after.

I left her with Sarah as I walked in with Sam. It's been a while since I had a proper catch up with him. We didn't get much of a chance yesterday due to my sombre mood. We headed to the Library as soon as we made it through the gates for some independent study time. I sit and listen as Sam tells me all about his application to University and how excited- if not nervous- he is for them to look it over and give him a decision. Sam then goes on to inform me of the holiday he has booked to Greece for the Summertime next year, but warns me 'it's a secret, tell Sarah and I'll cut your balls off!'

I tell Sam all about the cat coming out of the bag regarding Josie's true genetics. I tell him all about my Uncle not being my blood relation which causes Sam to place his hand on my shoulder supportively, he knows how close me and my Uncle are. I tell him that it doesn't change my relationship with my Uncle, but I do admit that it has made me feel slightly agitated because I thought mine and his relationship meant more to him than the truth he withheld. Sam sits silently, not knowing what to say. I'm okay with that, it's just nice to get all of this out in the open. It's been eating me inside since finding out, but Josie's had so much to deal with that I haven't wished to burden her with my own troubles. Sam also finds Josie's Stepmother's reaction odd, agreeing with me that if he were the one in this situation, he would be relieved for the truth to be out in the open, no longer having to pretend. Sam turns to me and asks if I regret approaching Josie and if I believe my life would have been easier if I'd just kept admiring her at a distance. It takes me a moment to answer him. I know he meant no menace by asking. Sam is a very hypothetical person; he likes to always ask 'what if?'

What would my life have been like? I'd still be a lonely person, meeting Sam here and there but remaining to keep myself to myself. Josie has opened my eyes to how vast the World is and just how much there is to explore. Without her, everything in my life is just split in half. She makes me whole. I tell Sam, with complete honesty: 'no'. Sam nods and smiles at me, telling me he feels exactly the same about Sarah.

When we run out of catching up, we both begin to start the work assigned to us. I plug my headphones in and zone out...

Chapter 17, Josie:

I'm midway through researching periodic behaviours when a Woman comes into the classroom, asking for me to go with her to the College Principal's office. Sarah shot me a look as I timidly got off my seat and grabbed my bag. I had no idea just what was about to hit me in the face. Can I not catch a fucking break? Lately, it just seems that when I am getting myself on track, life comes speeding around the corner to knock me off my feet screaming 'Ha, no enjoying me just yet Bitch!' From what I know, having to go to the College Principal is usually a sign of trouble. No one meets him unless he summons you, and it's usually not under friendly pretences. I say 'usually' because I could be wrong... I hope I'm wrong.

I knock on the dark grey door labelled *'Principal Anderson'* and wait for a response. After a suspenseful few seconds, I hear a gruff male voice beckoning me in.

"Ah, Ms. Martin, thank you for coming. I am so sorry for pulling you from your studies, but this is a matter that cannot wait. Please, take a seat." He points to a grey armchair opposite him. I'm noticing a grey theme with this office. I decide it's best not to speak until he carries on further. I sit myself to where he points and place my bag down beside me.

"I've just received a call from a very hysterical Lady, she said her name is Kat and she is your Stepmother?" Fuck... What the hell could she want that means she needs to get the College involved?

"She said she attempted to reach you on your mobile, but the number is out of service." Exactly the point of changing my phone number, so she cannot reach me. "It's your Dad, Ms. Martin. He's gone missing. Your Stepmother told me he left a note, but he hasn't been seen since yesterday afternoon." What. The. Fuck? Yesterday afternoon was when I told him- in as many words- that he is a shitty Father. Why would she bother going to the trouble of contacting the College for them to tell me this? I mean, she kept the fact that my Mother wasn't really dead from me, so why would she suddenly make me aware of this when it's miniscule in comparison to my Mother's 'death'? What am I expected to do? What can I do?

"Your Stepmother has requested you go to her so she can discuss the matter further with you. Thank you for meeting me Ms. Martin and I hope the issue is quickly resolved." It's like he read my mind, answering my silent questions. He looks at the door, dismissing me. So that's it? I expected our meeting to be longer. Then again, I never expected the reason behind his request to see me to be because of something like my Dad vanishing. I expected it to be because of my poor attendance as of late.

I make my way from the Principal's office and head towards the College gates. I pause momentarily to text Sarah, telling her I will not make it back to class. I politely ask her to take some notes for me and finish off by promising to update her later today. As I put my phone away, I realise I have to somehow tell Nick about my plans. I imagine it'll go down as well as a lead balloon. I decide it best not to tell him everything just yet and instead I text him informing him that I'm okay and telling him I love him. Way to go me, that won't raise any suspicions at all.

I am absolutely petrified of what I can expect as I make the journey to my Stepmother and Dad's.

~

'Kat,

Please forgive me for not being Man enough to say all of this to you face to face. I have replayed the words I will pour into this letter repeatedly. I wish there were an easier way to do this, but sadly it's all got too much now.

If you love someone, you must let them go. This is what I had to do with Martha and look how it all ended up. I have had time to reflect on what Josie said yesterday and I do strongly believe our relationship was built on vengeance rather than love. There has been numerous time over the past few years where I have questioned whether I could carry on... But I just can't anymore.

I should have been a better partner and a much better Father. Josie isn't biologically mine, but that doesn't mean she deserved the treatment we both dealt her since we forced Martha to leave. Josie may be Sal's kid by blood, but I watched that Girl grow. I was the one she called 'Daddy'. As we become parents, we strive to raise our Kids in a much better fashion than the way we, ourselves, were raised. I failed. I was raised abominably. No matter how much we beat Josie down, she kept getting back up and fighting for her happiness. My girl done me proud and I never got the chance to tell her so.

It's too late for me to apologise to her personally and honestly, I am far too cowardly to ever have been able to do so. It isn't too late for you though.... Be a better Woman. Stop letting the past haunt you. Out of the darkness that is the past came two beautiful rays of light: Maxie and Josie. Those two Girls shine so brightly and now Maxie will be bringing her own sunshine into everyone's lives. Be there for Maxie, she will need you. Swallow your bitterness and be the Grandmother Max will want you to be.

By the time you have read this letter, I plan to be long gone. Again Katrina, I am so sorry. Both of us together is a recipe for disaster, we fuel one another's evilness. I want to be better, that is why I am leaving so that one day, I can return a better person. I can finally try to be the Father I should have been from the very start.

Thank you for the good times, I will never forget those.

-    *Charlie x*

I read my Dad's letter twice over to be sure I'd read it right. He's proud of me. I never thought I'd hear or see those words come from him. The thought did cross my mind as I first begun to read it that this could be some sick joke of my Stepmothers. The writing is definitely my Dad's, it's so distinguishable that forging it would be neigh-on impossible to do. When I reached the house, my Stepmother had already opened the door. I'm guessing so she didn't have to open it for me and speak to me. I entered the house and found her standing at the bottom of the stairs, letter in hand. As I approached her, she thrust the folded piece of paper in my direction and as I took it from her, I remained keeping my wits about me. Someone who is unpredictable doesn't suddenly stop being unpredictable.

My Stepmother didn't move from the stairs as I read the letter, watching me intently. I look up at her to see her scowling at me. Without a word, she sticks her nose in the air and makes a swift exit to the lounge, closing the door behind her. I move to the stairs and perch, feeling too emotionally drained to try and leave just yet. My Stepmother will have to put up with me for a few minutes more while I attempt to collect myself. I am so numb that when my phone begins to buzz, I let it ring off. I know it will be Nick and I can't deal with his questions right now.

My Dad is correct... he is a coward. He had multiple opportunities to stand up for me, but never did. Even if he didn't really want to, he still stood by my Stepmother as she unleashed all sorts of hell on me. I was strong enough to get through the past few years of abuse and torture I endured, but to think there are others out there going through the same thing who may not be as strong as I am, is sickening. The thing is, my Dad never even let on that he was on my side, or that he did feel some sort of love for me. He had opportunities to take me to the side, or to come and find me to tell me that he didn't agree with my Stepmother's actions. Instead, he led me to believe all along that he was as bad as she was and still is. He is wrong for standing by and watching, but I would have had less hatred towards him if he tried. Even when it was just me and him- the rare few times we did have to ourselves- he was still cold towards me. I can't remember having a proper conversation with him since coming to live with him. Before my Stepmother, our relationship was good. Of course, now I fully know everything, I know why he and my Stepmother acted the way they did. I hope wherever he is, he's safe. I hope that he is true to his word and returns a better man. Charlie Martin is not a bad man he just made bad decisions and, in my eyes, that does not automatically make someone bad. What a person does and who a person is should not be confused with how pure it makes them.

My phone buzzing again breaks me from my trance. Nick again... I roll my eyes as I pluck my phone from the front pocket of my bag. Yep, Nick. I swipe up to answer it and place the phone to my ear. I already know he'll begin ranting at me before I have the chance to speak, so I remain silent as I answer. Again, I am right. Call it intuition or just something I have grown used to from being in awkward situations a million fucking times now!

"Josie? Where are you? Are you okay? Why did you leave College? I came to find you and you weren't there. Sarah showed me the text. Why couldn't you go back to class? Why were you removed from class? Again, where are you? Please tell me you went home because you were unwell or something." He doesn't even draw a breath as he fires twenty-one questions at me.

"I'm okay. I'm at my Stepmother's. It's- "

"WHAT? WHY?" Nick rudely cuts me off before I have a chance to explain.

"If you can let me finish before you butt in... My Dad has left. No one knows where he's gone but he left a letter. My Stepmother rung the College and asked for me. I had no choice Nick. He's my Dad."

"Firstly, I am not apologising for cutting you off. Secondly, why do you care? You should rejoice that the old fart has fucked off! You owe nothing to your Stepmother, Josie. That Woman should be behind bars for the things she has put you through and the pain she has inflicted on you. I'm not buying any of this, something feels off. Oh, and he isn't your Dad, so as well as not owing anything to your Stepmother, you also owe him nothing." *Ouch*.

"Low blow, Nick. I know when I'm being played and right now, I can confidently say that I am not being played!" As I say these words, I can't be sure I believe them. There always seems to be some sort of hidden meaning behind my Stepmother's actions...

"Stop being naïve! You have enough people around you that can hand on heart say they love and care for you. You don't need either of those shitty excuses for parents!" I'm on the verge of falling apart. Nick's just being truthful but right now the truth seems to be biting me on the arse, hard. For once, I think I'd appreciate being lied to. At least lies only hurt if they are uncovered.

"I'm going to go. You're pissed and I get that but right now, I need some time with my thoughts. I just read that my Dad is proud of me, Nick. I know that may be hard to believe but to actually read it stirs all sorts of emotions in me. I'll go home in a second. I love you." I hang up, avoiding having to listen to Nick protest. He would want me to go home right this moment, but I want to speak to my Stepmother before I do so. I didn't add that detail into my conversation with Nick because I knew if I had, he'd personally come here and drag me out whether I wanted him to or not. I know he's just trying to keep me safe, but I can handle myself. I head to the lounge but find the door open and the room vacant. My stepmother must have moved whilst I was on the phone as I didn't hear her leave.

A clatter from within the Kitchen quickly gives her location away. I shuffle towards the Kitchen door and stand awkwardly. She has her back to me as she rummages through a cupboard. I clear my throat and she turns to face me, the frown she held earlier still prominent across her forehead.

"Thank you for the letter. I'm going to head off now. I hope wherever my Dad is, he's okay. I hope you're okay." I wasn't too sure what to say but thankfully my brain and mouth were connected for once, so I didn't have to search for the right sentence to string together.

My Stepmother just nods at me in response. I take that as the only sort of response I will receive so I turn from the Kitchen and head back to the stairs to retrieve my bag. After yesterday I vowed never to step back through the front door to this house, but for the second time in two days I leave, choosing to close the door silently this time.

~

I decided to walk home. It was a trek, but it was needed. The crunch of the orange and red leaves beneath my feet was therapeutic. There's something about Autumn that just feels magical. There's a particular spark still present in the air from the excitement of the Summer drawing to a close.

Home comes into view and I start to drag my feet slightly, knowing that Nick shaped wrath is most likely standing behind the front door. I don't intentionally piss him off, but we do differ in opinion on many things. Usually it's because I believe to be doing the right thing for me. He's always right in the end but I wouldn't openly admit that to him. Being told you are right is always something to gloat about and I am too stubborn to give him the satisfaction.

I place my key into the lock and I'm thankful when the door isn't pulled open, that's a start. As quietly as the door will allow, I step inside. I'm relieved when my first sight isn't of Nick with his arms folded over his chest. As I'm beginning to wonder where he could be, I hear a beeping noise coming from below me. Someone is in the gym and seeing as Nick's Uncle isn't home at the moment, it can only be Nick. I spend a minute debating whether to go down there or not, but eventually I decide not to. He is more than likely burning off some steam. Steam that I have caused.

I head to the Kitchen for some much-needed caffeine. My phone buzzes and I snatch it up to see a message from Sarah:

'Hey Lovely, I hope everything is okay. Nick was pissed that you hadn't

messaged him. He was pretty persistent, so I didn't have much choice but to show him the message you had sent me. I feel like I should lose some friend points for being so weak and giving in so easily. Honestly though, I hope everything is okay. Message me when you get the chance. Love ya xxx'

Bless her. I know what a persistent Nick is like, poor her for being on the receiving end of it. She doesn't lose any friend points for that; she can always repay me with a coffee in the morning.

I'm in the process of conjuring up a reply in my head when a sweaty, gym clothed Nick comes into view. I try to not be so obvious, but I can't help how my eyes scan his body. He's breathing hard. All coherent thoughts quickly leave my mind. The tension is so thick you could cut it with a knife.

"Coffee?" Wow. That's the best I can offer... I give myself a mental slap to the face. Nick sweeps his tongue across his bottom lip and rolls his eyes at my offer. He places his hands on the back of one of the bar stools, his grip so tight that his knuckles turn white. I swallow hard at the unpredictably of his mood.

"No, Josie. No. I don't want any fucking coffee. I want some answers. Do you honestly have no regard for your own safety? You went running to your Stepmother at her first command since you left there. Have you completely forgotten what she did to you?" Nick manages to keep his voice controlled but I can feel the anger radiating from him, despite being about ten feet away from one another. I don't immediately answer him, carefully drafting an answer before I respond so I don't come out with anything stupid.

"I didn't go running as you so pleasantly put it. She didn't even give any command. I chose to go there because I was told my Dad had vanished and left nothing but a note. If you want to know what my thought process was... well I thought the note was a suicide note. I know that's so dark but that's usually why notes are left. I didn't mean to just leave without telling you, but I knew how you'd react. You'd tell me not to go. I haven't forgotten what happened to me, I replay that shit in my head daily. I have nightmares every single night, reliving the things that happened to me. But I am an adult Nick. You don't need to accompany me everywhere as if you're my bodyguard. I'm not some defenceless animal." Shit. The speech I had come up with was nothing quite as bad as what actually just came out of my mouth. My brain and mouth were definitely not connected in that moment. I'm breathless and Nick is speechless. His brows are knitted so closely together that they are so close to touching. He is gripping the back of the bar stool so harshly that it squeaks. I turn my back and continue making my coffee. I daren't look around.

As I'm spooning sugar into the mug, I suddenly feel a breath of hot air on the nape of my neck. Before I have a chance to react, I am grabbed by the waist and hoisted onto the kitchen counter. Nick parts my legs and takes his place between them, placing his hands on the cupboard overheard so that I am trapped in. He leans his face as close to mine as he can. His gaze is so intense that I look down.

"You drive me crazy; you know that? You've been conditioned to believe you are not worthy of being cared for. You may not need a bodyguard, but you sure as hell need someone to show they give a shit about what happens to you. How observant of you to tell me that you are an adult, how would I have ever known should you not have informed me of that fact." What a funny arse. "You are always free to do whatever it is your heart desires, but I WILL step in if I believe the situation could cause you physical or emotional harm. Was a simple text too much to ask? Poor Sarah looked like she wanted to kill me when I eventually got her to share your text with me. Josie will you please look at me. When you look down it makes me feel that you're afraid of me. Please never be afraid of me. Please..." Nick's voice goes from certain to small as he finishes his speech. His plea pulls my heart apart and I immediately look up into his eyes. I cup his face between my hands and he visibly relaxes but keeps his hands either side of my head, keeping me caged in.

"I'm sorry. Next time I'll text you first. I promise."

"Next time? Sweetheart, there WILL NOT be a next time. I will not let you be alone with that Woman ever again. Do you genuinely believe that she wouldn't hurt you again just because you no longer reside there? She's an abuser, Josie. Abusers are practically reptiles; they have no emotion and they do not care about hurting someone over and over again until they have completely broken them. They will carry on until they hold someone's soul and then, whilst the person looks on, they will crush the soul in their hand." Hot tears make their way down my cheeks. I know he's right, but it doesn't make it any less hard to hear. Part of me believes my Stepmother can be changed. She has a heart somewhere beneath that hard exterior. She must...

Nick removes one hand from above me and uses the pad of his thumb to swipe the tears from my face. He observes me with eyes full of adoration.

"I really don't have the energy to fight with you anymore. My Dad may have always appeared to have had no love or respect for me, but it wasn't the same way for me. I loved him because I remembered the man he was before he turned cold and unforgiveable. You can't keep me safe forever, no matter how much you want to. There is always going to be something or someone out to cause harm. I love that you care about me so much and to be truthful, it's been hard adapting to having someone care about me and what I'm up to." I have so much more to say but the ticks in Nick's jaw are becoming closer together. I know he's mad, but he isn't mad at me. He's mad because I have shitty excuses for parents, and they seem to be worming their way into my life far too much. I knew I wouldn't just be able to walk away and that would be final. Nick's right (again...), my Stepmother is an abuser, and abusers will continue to fuck with their victims long after the victim believes they have escaped their clutches.

"I didn't think we were fighting. It shouldn't matter who your Dad used to be. That Man is long gone, and you've had to deal with this new version. A version of your Dad that IS unforgiveable. I hope he has left to go somewhere far away because if I ever see that weak, pathetic excuse of a Man again, I will not be able to restrain myself from acting on the rage I feel towards him. He stood by and watched every beating; he heard every harsh word and he never supported a single thing you did or wanted to do. Are you forgetting what he said to you about going to University? Any normal parent would have been so proud of their kid. Not him... No, instead he belittled you. He made you feel incapable of making it to University, despite knowing just how intelligent you are. For all I care, he can rot in hell." I swallow the hard lump in my throat to prevent further tears spilling down my cheek.

Nick has moved past being angry and has gone straight to unreasonable and cruel.

"So, what is this then, a happy exchange between us? Jesus, Nick. He was proud of me. He was just so blindsided by his love for my Stepmother he would ask 'how high' if she told him to jump. My old Dad was still in there, but he was being held prisoner. He was probably scared of my Stepmother. She's a scary Woman, Nick. She brings even the strongest to their knees at a simple glance. My Dad wanted me to know he was proud of me, that's why he put it in his letter. He admitted his weakness." I've begun to shake with the force of holding back my tears. I dare to steal a glance into Nick's eyes. If it were possible for eyes to be ablaze, Nick's certainly would be. They are full of fury. I don't know how much further he can be pushed before he snaps.

He pushes off from the cupboards but remains stood between my legs. His hands go to his hair and he tilts his head backwards, taking a deep breath as he does so. There's a few seconds of tense silence. Nick keeps his head pointed at the ceiling and I stay rooted to where I am sat on the Kitchen counter. We are inches from one another but yet we are so far.

"Why are you defending him, Josie?" Nick's voice is silent, and I have to strain to hear him properly.

"Huh?" I knew I heard him right, but I need to hear it again.

"I asked why you're defending him? After everything... Why are you painting him out to be a fucking hero?" My composure is gone. I shove Nick and he stumbles backwards slightly, shocked by my sudden action. I jump down from the counter and begin to storm from the Kitchen. I don't make it far, but I guessed I wouldn't. I feel Nick's hand on my elbow, gripping me in a way so as not to hurt me but to keep me from walking any further from him.

"JOSIE!" His voice booms and my eardrums vibrate. I flinch and hear Nick's sharp intake of breath. He doesn't want me to be scared of him but I'm so conditioned to associate loud voices with negative outcomes.

"I'm not defending him! I will never, EVER, forgive him for allowing me to be abused as he watched on. He is my Dad. Do you know what it's like to pine for someone? I thought my Mum was dead and all I wanted was my Dad to just… be there. For him to be my Dad. So, to read those words after years of wishing for them, it's as if all of my Christmases came at once." I fully break after my last word is uttered. I shrug myself from Nick's grasp so I can place my hands over my face and sob. I move to the corner of the room and slide down the wall. My eyes are so blurred that I can't make out Nick's expression, but thankfully he has chosen to stay quiet. It doesn't take long for Nick to rush to my side, encasing me in his arms and hugging me to his chest.

"Shh, baby. It's okay. I'm sorry, I didn't mean to upset you so badly. I just couldn't understand because I've been viewing everything through my own eyes and not putting myself in your shoes, but I get it. I know it's slightly different but if my Dad came back into the picture, I would probably forgive his multitude of sins. We're not supposed to hate our parents. Come on, stand with me. I'm going to take you out for dinner, you deserve a distraction from everything." Nick releases me to stand, holding his hands out to me. When we're both stood in front of one another, Nick proceeds to dry the leftover tears from my face and then places a kiss on my forehead.

We both head upstairs together to get changed for dinner. Butter-flies make their way into my stomach; I've never been out to dinner with a guy before. This is a proper date!

I opt for a navy-blue pencil dress and black heels. I rummage through my cardigans and jackets, trying to find one that will go with my dress. It isn't particularly cold out, but of an evening it isn't exactly warm. I find a black knitted shawl and fling it over my shoulders. I decide to apply my makeup as naturally as I can, only applying a thin line of black eyeliner and coating my lashes in black mascara. I cover the small number of blemishes on my face with concealer but decide not to add anything else. I battle between whether to wear my hair up in a low bun or to curl it. Low bun wins the battle, but I leave a few strands free around the front. I critique myself in the floor length mirror and, satisfied that I look suitable for my first ever date, I grab my black clutch from the bottom of my wardrobe and head out of my bedroom.

Nick comes into view as I reach the top of the stairs and I feel my pupils dilate at the sight of him. He is wearing black dress trousers with a pair of brown, suede shoes. He wears the whitest shirt I have ever seen, leaving a few buttons open so that part of his Stag head tattoo peeks through. He wears a black blazer with the sleeves partly rolled up, exposing a few of the many tattoos inked on his arms. He looks... delicious. Yeah, delicious... That's the only word I can come up with. Nick winks at me as I reach the bottom of the stairs and he offers me his arm which I take a hold of without a second thought.

Chapter 18, Nick:

"So, your first ever kiss was with a boy two years younger than you? Such a cougar!" Josie playfully swats my arm as I tease her. Dinner was amazing and we both got over our nerves quick enough to have a good time. Our starter consisted of a Prawn Cocktail, for our main course I opted for a medium rare steak while Josie chose a Carbonara, and for dessert we both decided to share a brownie. I felt that our dinner date flew by a bit too quickly, so I asked Josie to let me show her one of my favourite places. She agreed without hesitation.

One of my favourite places is a small garden-like area a short walk from the restaurant we came from. In the middle is a gazebo type building. It reminds me a bit of the last scene from the first 'Twilight' film, where Edward takes Bella to dance under the illusion that he will turn her into a Vampire. Sadly, I am not a Vampire and we are not in 'Twilight', but it does look exactly the same as the one from the film. The Gazebo is surrounded by rows of Rose bushes and in the evening, solar panelled lights illuminate all around. Many couples come here for dates and many a romantic sonnet has been uttered here. This place holds a sort of magic to it which can be felt in the air just as it can be seen with the eye. I glance down to my Girl to find her absolutely mesmerised by the view in front of us. As she admires her view, I admire mine. Josie's eyes are lit by the small fairy lights above us, making them sparkle in the most glorious of ways. The lights beam down on Josie's face, illuminating her face with a soft orange glow. Her mouth is open as she gawps in awe, tilting her head slightly as she takes in the view. She mouths 'beautiful' as she continues to observe. Yes, you are Josie...

I hold my hand out in front of her, palm facing upwards. Josie stares at me.

"May I have this dance?" Josie grins and gives me a small curtsey, placing her hand in mine. I walk us both to the middle of the light wood flooring of the Gazebo, just as a few droplets of rain hit my face. Thankfully the Gazebo is sheltered.

I click my heels together and bow at Josie, bowing at my Queen. She blushes but giggles at my romantic gesture. I take her hand and place it on my shoulder. My hand falls to her waist and our free hands find one another's and we grip them together tightly.

There's no music but we manage to find our own rhythm. There's no doubt about it, one day I will be proposing to this Girl in this very spot. I once called this place 'my place', the place where I would come to think or where I would sit by myself with headphones and a book. It's no longer *my place*, it's ours...

~

We looked like a couple of drowned rats when we made it back home. The rain had started to pelt down by the time we were all danced out. I had pulled my phone from my blazer pocket to call us a cab, but Josie refused. I was left with no chance of reluctance before I was being pulled from the Gazebo and into the heavy shower. I made no attempts to hide my distaste at being forced to walk in the rain. Josie had laughed me off and skipped a few paces ahead of me, twirling with her arms extended. Watching her be so carefree was enough to rid me of my mood.

I run us a hot bath as Josie makes Hot Chocolate. That girl makes a mean cup of cocoa! She goes all out with whipped cream and marshmallows.

The bath is run but there's still no sign of Josie. I call her name but get no response. What is she doing? Leaving the bathroom, I stop to listen around. Light illuminates from my bedroom, giving away Josie's whereabouts. My mouth dries at the thought of her waiting naked on my bed. Seductive thoughts are very quickly replaced with a feeling of dread as I hear Josie sobbing. This isn't just any sort of crying either, it's one of anguish... I speed walk along the remainder of the hall to my room.

Chapter 19, Josie:

Tonight was magical. I'd forgotten what it was like to be able to switch off from the World and live in the moment. Tonight made me certain that I will never want anyone else but Nick. But of course, the clock struck Midnight and my bliss turned into a nightmare.

During mine and Nick's date, I had switched my phone off. The first stomach dropping feeling that something was off was the swarm of missed calls from Maxie. My immediate thoughts were about the baby and I wasted little time in calling Max back. She answered on the second ring, her voice coming through the speaker in a rush.

"Where have you been? I've been trying you all evening! Josie, something's happened. Something bad. I didn't want my Mum to get to you first, she wouldn't be delicate in telling you the news..." Bile rises in my throat at the endless possibilities swimming through my head.

"Maxie, out with it."

"Your Dad's dead," she mummers, but I heard her loud and clear. My throat tightens and my pulse quickens. I haven't had a panic attack in a while now and I certainly do not welcome the one that threatens to make an appearance now. How can my Dad be dead?

"What happened," I ask Maxie, my voice barely a whisper.

"I found him at the bottom of the stairs. He must have tripped, no one knows for sure. I wasn't here, I'd just got back from James's. Mum told me she hadn't been in all day. It was an accident," Max sounds so sure.

"When did he come back? I literally came round earlier to read the letter he wrote. He said he was going away."

"What letter? Josie, what are you talking about? He never left. Mum never mentioned any letter." What.

"What do you mean, he didn't leave? He left a letter clearly stating that he had to leave. Have you not seen it?"

"No… Mum would've said but he's been here the whole time," Max quizzes me. Am I going mad? What the hell is going on?

"Max, I'm going to head off and process everything. I'll message you tomorrow and we can meet. I love you, stay safe." I end the call and toss my phone on the Kitchen counter. The two mugs full of Hot Chocolate steam in front of me but for once the smell isn't soothing or inviting.

I don't remember the walk up the stairs or how I ended up in Nick's bedroom, but somehow, I did. I collapse on to his bed and hug Nick's pillow to me. The numbness makes it way through me, coursing through my veins alongside my blood. At the end of the hall, I hear Nick calling for me, but the sound is distorted. I make no attempts to move and keep my head buried in the pillow beneath me. The next thing I know, Nick is stood in the doorway and he looks at me with eyes full of concern. I just stare at him, feeling dead inside. If that letter isn't real then everything was a lie. But why would the letter be fake? It was my Dad's handwriting I'm sure of it. The bed dips as Nick gets in with me. He doesn't say anything, he just traces his finger up and down my bicep. The dress from our date still clings to me from the damp rain but that isn't the reason I'm shivering.

I'm shivering because I'm scared… Because nothing is what it seems and I just keep ending up hurt. What's the point of being a good person if you constantly get hurt? What is the fucking point?

"What's happened, Baby?" Nick asks softly.

"My Dad died, but that isn't the worst part. I feel awful for saying so but it truly isn't the worst part of it all," I feel so horrible but I'm not lying, the deceit is the worst part of it. It's the part that hurts the most.

"Shit. When? How?" Nick asks.

"I don't really want to go into specifics. I just want to be left alone. Please," I mean it, I just want everyone to leave me alone so I can catch a break.

"You know me better than that. I'm not leaving you alone in this state. For one, you'll catch a cold if you stay in that dress much longer," Nick softly tells me. Before I can argue, he scoops me into his arms, and I'm carried to the bathroom where the most luscious looking bath meets my eyes. Nick places me gently on my feet and begins peeling my dress from my body. There's nothing inappropriate about this, he is careful, treating me delicately. When I'm bare, Nick scoops me up again and gently lowers me into the Bathtub. He twirls my hair into a bun and secures it with a hair tie so he can begin to wash my back. I remain staring blankly ahead, the only thing I seem to be able to do at the moment.

After the bath, Nick goes to the Kitchen to make the hot drinks that I should've made, and I climb into his bed.

~

'I stare into cold, unforgiving eyes. The blade clasped in her pale, bony hand. Her sharp, claw-like painted black nails a striking contrast against her ivory complexion.

I regret coming here now. I should have stayed away but, in true 'Martin' form, I cannot just accept things for how they are. I've spent my whole life with my eyes forced closed and now they have opened, I have no way of shutting them again. Knowing what I know has led me straight into the Lion's Den and the Lioness is in front of me, waiting to pounce.

Inhaling a shaky breath and balling my hands into fists, I take another step towards her. Her mouth twisting up in the most feral, sinister *smile. The blade in her hand glinting against the dim light.*

There is no escape.

~

I sit up sharply in bed, my hair stuck to my forehead and my heart hammering so hard against my ribs that it threatens to break free.

"Hey, it's okay, it was just a nightmare, you're safe," Nick brushes my hair from my forehead and places small kisses along my shoulder.

I lay my head back on the pillow and take deep breaths to attempt to slow my heart rate. What in the world was that nightmare? I've never ended up having a dream so dark, usually I just replay things from the past and the only severity level they reach is when I wake up with a few tears. This was pure terror. The woman smiling at me so vindictively had resembled my Stepmother but yet, she wasn't quite my Stepmother. Her eyes were exactly the same: cold and unforgiving.

Nick keeps his eyes on me, probably worrying that I'll fall apart should he look away.

I lay my head into the crook of his arm, entwining my legs with his and begging for a blissful sleep to take over.

~

The dark circles under my eyes give away the sort of night I had, I wish I could spend the whole day in bed catching up on the sleep that I had stolen from me, but I needed to see Maxie. I called her a matter of minutes after waking up, asking her to come here. She was more than happy to, knowing that I couldn't bring myself to go to her and have to face my Stepmother. There's a tiny part of me that feels obligated to check on my Stepmother and make sure she is holding up. She must have felt some sort of love for my Dad. People don't stick around for that length of time if they don't have some sort of feelings, right?

The door knocks and I shout for Maxie to come in. I've made a coffee for myself and a decaf tea for Max. She walks into the Kitchen and I rush to her. We share the warmest and most sincerest hug I think we've ever shared. We're both hurting. He was Max's Stepdad after all... She has just as much right to hurt as the rest of us. He was never horrible to her. Max got the Dad I wanted, but I hold no resentment towards her. I couldn't bear it if she had also had to endure what I did. I pat her softly on the back before I break away. Leading us to the lounge with our drinks, we sink down onto the sofa.

I figure it's best to get the tough questions out of the way.

"Did you really mean it when you said there wasn't a letter? I'm not insane Max, I read it twice and it was my Dad's handwriting. He wasn't there when I got there, it was just your Mum. She even got in contact with the College because she had no other way of reaching me. Something isn't right. Please tell me I'm not going insane," I plead with Maxie.

"I honestly wish I had the answers but I truthfully don't. It's all a bit odd to me but I'm serious when I say I do believe you. My mum does some questionable things but- and not like I'm defending her- but to forge a letter is a bit steep, even for her."

"God, it just doesn't make sense! It is steep and just down right weird to think she could have anything to do with this. I'm just left questioning how true anything is... Like, is he really dead? Is this just another coy to make me feel even more insane when he suddenly reappears," My last sentence came out more spiteful than I intended it to and Max winces. My frustration isn't intentionally aimed at her but I can't help as it bubbles over the surface. I need answers; I need closure.

"He is, Josie. This isn't some sick prank. I leant down and felt for his pulse and there wasn't one. I'll never get the image of him lying there out of my head," she begins to cry and I immediately feel like an absolute bitch. Shuffling to her, I bring her head to my chest and hold her against me, allowing her to accept her hurt and to pour it all out. I wonder if she's been able to cry like this with my Stepmother.

"I'm sorry Moo, I really am... I didn't mean to purposely make you upset. I guess I'm just used to being able to release all of my anger on to Nick but he's deliberately staying away to give us this quality time to talk. It's never an excuse to take out personal hurt on someone else, especially when you're not at fault for all of this occurring. I'm so sorry," I tell Maxie in my sincerest and most gentle tone.

Moo is the name I gave Maxie when we first met. She had a little stuffed toy of a Cow, and when you pressed it's belly you was rewarded with a 'moo'. It used to make us giggle and we drove our Parents insane with it. The speaker eventually broke, but Max kept hold of the toy. It now resides on a shelf in her bedroom, but she doesn't mind her nickname.

"It's okay, I know why you're angry and I would be too. You're not mad, Jo. I just wish I had some sort of answer for you. Do you think seeing your Dad would make you feel any sort of closure or would it be too tough? I get if it would... If I'd known my Dad properly, I would find it hard to see him. I know the Funeral Home he's in... I can come with you, if you want to go that is?" Max is right, it would be hard for me to see him lying there, cold and unmoving. But it would bring me some sort of closure. I believe there's something after this life... I'm not too sure what, but I believe there's something. This could be the only time I get to tell my Dad how I feel about him before I never get that chance again in this lifetime. I believe he'll hear me in spirit. I need to see him.

"I would like to go, and I'd appreciate the company. I have so much I need to say to him," my voice cracks and tears threaten to spill but I choke them back. I'm so sick of crying. Suddenly, an idea crosses my mind, but I have no idea what Max would make of it...

"Moo, how would you feel about speaking to your Dad again? It's too late for me to make things right with my Dad, but you still have a chance to get to know him. He's actually a really nice guy,

I mean look at what he did for Nick. I know he left you and your Mum without a second thought but I know it still affects him," Max stills beside me. She'd been twirling a ring around her index finger but the shock of hearing me suggest such a thing brings her to a standstill.

"Would you be there with me if I do? I don't resent my Dad for leaving us. My Mum is hard work and now you've explained their history, I understand why he felt leaving was the right thing to do. A few years ago now, on my birthday, I was in the Kitchen and as I went to put something in the bin, a red envelope caught my eye. I'd already opened my cards and there hadn't been a red envelope amongst them. I fished it out and opened it... It was from my Dad. Mum threw it away. I hid it up my shirt and opened it in the bathroom. He's sent cards every single year and Mum just threw them away. He's never forgotten me, Jo. I've just had no way of contacting him," she's quiet as she reveals this to me. Sal didn't deserve that. He should have been allowed to contact his own Daughter and to have been able to send a birthday card without it being tossed. My Stepmother had no right to be so cruel.

"Well, I think he'd love to see you again. Do you want his number or would you rather I arrange a meeting?"

"Could you arrange a meeting, please? I have no idea what I'd say if I messaged him first."

"Of course I can. He'll be over the moon to find out about the Baby. I'll leave that little surprise for you to reveal," I wink at her and she laughs, placing her hand over her belly.

"I can't wait to find out if I'm having a little Girl or a little Boy. I don't care about the gender, as long as it's healthy. That's all anyone can hope for really," Max beams with pride and I realise just how proud I am of her. She'll be an amazing Mum and James will be an excellent Dad. If you were to type 'match made in Heaven' into Google, James and Maxie's names would appear.

"I will be with you every step of the way. I'll just be the fun Aunt who turns up drunk to every event," I smirk at her.

"Oh I'm counting on it! If you're okay, I'm going to leave and make some arrangements with the Funeral home for a visit as soon as possible so you can say goodbye to your Dad," my heart sinks at the word 'goodbye'. It's so final.

"I'm okay Moo, as long as you are. Thank you for doing this for me. I'll call Sal tonight and arrange a time for you guys to meet. I'll message you right away, I promise," Max squeezes my hand in response and stands, readying herself to leave.

We both walk to the front door and exchange a long, meaningful hug. As soon as I close the door, the dread finally hits me. Nick appears at the top of the stairs just in time to see me slide to the floor with my head in my hands.

Chapter 20, Nick:

The sight before me breaks me in half. My beautiful girl, so broken and small. It took all my self control to stay away during Maxie's visit. I knew Josie would find today difficult but I found some solace in knowing that the two Girls on the floor below me would be able to comfort one another. Their relationship really makes me wish I had a sibling; someone I could've shared life with from the very start.

The sound of the front door closing had me leaping from my bed and hurrying across the hall to the top of the stairs. Josie looked up at me from below, her eyes glazed over and a haunted look on her face. She squeezed her eyes tightly shut and buried her face in her hands.

Rushing to her, I swept her up from the floor and carried her to the safety of the sofa. My Girl is a Queen, and Queens do not belong on the floor, no matter the circumstance.

I allowed her some breathing room and made my way to the Kitchen to make her a Coffee.

Now, back in the Lounge, I beg her to tell me what happened. What had caused this look to invade her striking features?

Josie tells me of the impending visit to the Funeral Home. She opens up and bears her soul as she discusses the terror she feels. Josie feels everything is too final and she has regrets about the things she left unsaid. I kiss her forehead, reminding her that she was never allowed the chance to open up to her Dad, she isn't at fault for that. I ask to go with her to the Funeral Home so I can support her and she nods her head instantly. She politely asked that I stay out of the room while she says her last goodbyes, something I respect, of course.

I once read a quote: *'when life gets tough, remind yourself that strong walls shake but never collapse'.* This is Josie. She has been shook by so much but she still faces the world each and every day with a smile.

Chapter 21, Josie:

Four days later:

This is it. The pinnacle moment I have been dreading. Every night leading up to this, I have had the most haunting nightmares. In them, I find myself walking down a dark corridor of a morgue. As I near a dimly lit room, I notice a body on the table right in front of me. I near the body to discover it is my Dad. I hover my hand over his body as a single tear rolls down my cheek. Just a I turn to walk away, a hand shoots out from under the pure white cover and catches my hand in a vice like grip. I try to scream but no sound comes out. That's when I wake up, drenched and struggling to breathe.

The Funeral Home is nothing like my nightmares, thank God. Instead, the smell of fresh flowers penetrates my sense of smell and the colour black is kept minimal. I'm led to the Chapel of Rest. The Funeral Director gives my shoulder a squeeze and re-assures me they will be right outside with any questions. I slowly walk towards the catafalque, taking deep breaths in and out to calm my nerves. I had a whole speech prepared, but the minute I stepped foot into the Funeral Directors, it all went straight out the window.

My Dad looks so calm... So at peace. For the first time in his life, he is carefree. He just looks like he's sleeping.

"Hey Dad umm... It's me... It's Josie. You know that, of course," I let out a nervous chuckle. "God, there's so much I want to say to you but now I'm actually here, it's so hard to get it all out and I don't want to cry. I hope you're someplace happy... I read a note. I was so sure it was from you but now, I'm not so sure. In that 'note' you told me you're proud of me but you was just never able to tell me to my face. I wanted to make you proud. More than anything. You were my Dad... You raised me and, even after finding out the stuff I did, I still couldn't come to terms that you weren't my real Dad. I couldn't find it in myself to strip you of that title. Through all the bad, there were so many good times we shared. Remember that one time when I accidentally bounced off of my bed and hit my head on the wall, you absolutely wet yourself over it," I stop to let out a sob and swipe tears away from my face. "I want you to know that I carry no resentment towards you for anything you did. I wish you'd been there for me just a little bit more, but I know what it's like to be in someone's clutches so much that you second guess everything you do. It's not an excuse, but I do understand. I can't help but just feel so angry... Angry at life and the way it works. Like, these amazing people are placed into your world and you grow to love them with everything you have... Only for it to be ripped away from you. It leaves you questioning why anyone bothers falling in love or why people bother having close relationships. There's a saying: 'It's an honour and a blessing to have something that makes saying goodbye so hard'. How true it is... So I guess what I really wanted to say, Dad is... I forgive you for everything, because if I hadn't gone through the things I have, I would never have wound up at a party where I would meet the love of my life. I would never have learnt to treat others with kindness or have learnt to love myself for who I am. One day, you'll be a Grandad in another life and I hope you can look down on your Grandkids with pride. Please just promise that you'll be there in spirit to walk me down the isle?" I choke again on another sob at the realisation of all the things my Dad will not be there for; the important milestones in my life. "I love you so much, Dad. I always have, and I always will. See you again," with that, I place my hand over his and lean down to kiss his cheek. Just as I turn to leave, a tidal wave of emotion hits me right in the chest, and I perch on a seat to collect myself. I hope he heard me, wherever he is...

A week and a half later: the funeral...

I give myself a last minute check over in the mirror before I have to leave. Dressed in black from head to toe in a lace, high neck skater dress, a black cardigan and low heeled court shoes, I feel as empty as the morbid colour that hangs from me. My eyes are dark and sunken from a sleepless night of crying into my pillow and my hands will not stop shaking. Nick has been as supportive as he always is, staying up with me all night to hold me tight. He looks just as done in as I do. Nick still holds a small amount of resentment for my Father, but out of respect for me I know he's pushed it to the side.

Nick's Uncle waits for us at the bottom of the stairs to drive us to my Stepmother's where the car will be waiting to escort myself, my Stepmother, Max and Nick to the Funeral. My Mum will also be in attendance, causing the anxiety eating away at me to multiply. It isn't my Mum I'm worried about... It's how my Stepmother will react to her presence. I hope they can keep the claws away just for today. My Mum was in pieces when she found out about my Dad. There was a time where she did love him and she also holds happy memories, so she has a right to be there today.

We arrive at the house, Nick grips my hand tighter as my Stepmother comes into view. Of course, she is as pristine as they come. She wears a knee length, black pencil dress, a pair of black high heels, a coat which just screams 'I'm a very important person', and a black headpiece with lace covering her eyes. She dabs her eyes dramatically despite there being no evidence of tear stains on her heavily made up face.

Nick's elbow gently pokes me in the side and I realise I've been scowling at my Stepmother from the moment I laid eyes on her.

Without a word, we step out of one vehicle and into another. The only communication is between myself and Max as we exchange a brief side hug.

~

The Funeral begins and my Dad's coffin is carried in to his favourite song: 'Always' by Bon Jovi. The coffin bearers bow in respect and leave. My Stepmother decided on a cremation for my Dad, probably so she didn't have to stand with us should she have chosen a burial. Over the past week I have offered numerous times to help towards the Funeral or the wake, but my Stepmother shut me down harshly each time, telling me 'she doesn't need my charity'. As if it's fucking charity. I've kept the texts between us just in case she ever decides to throw my lack of contribution in my face.

So far, my Stepmother and my Mum haven't acknowledged one another and I've never been more grateful.

The service went far too quickly and I looked down at the ground as the curtain closed around my Dad's coffin. The finale of my Dad's short time on this Earth.

The wake was held at a my Dad's favourite bar. The event room adjacent had been hired out for the afternoon by my Stepmother. I take in the vastness of the room; a buffet takes up the majority of the room and photographs of my Dad stand proud on each surface. I notice that of all the many photos in the room, there isn't a single one of my Dad and me, however there's plenty of my Dad with my Stepmother and Max. My Stepmother decided to be vicious down to the last minute. I swallow my hate down, reminding myself that after today I can cut all ties with her. I head back to the bar where Nick stands chatting to my Mum. My Mum pulls me into a tight embrace as I near.

"Josie Bear, you've really picked a diamond! I'm so proud to call this lad my son in law," my Mum beams at me with pride.

"I know Mum, I picked the best of the best," I smugly respond, tapping Nick playfully on the shoulder.

"I know this isn't the best place to have this conversation, but I would love for us to try and mend bridges, that is if I haven't burnt every single one," my Mum looks at me nervously. She's my Mum. After losing Dad so suddenly, I've come to appreciate each second of life.

"I would like that," I smile back at her and her face lights up in excitement.

"I have to use the bathroom, I'll be back in a minute," I excuse myself and my Mum and Nick continue their discussion.

The Women's bathroom is joined to the events room by a small corridor. I push the door open to find there are two cubicles, two sinks and two hand dryers. One stall is already occupied so I make my way into the empty cubicle. A few seconds after I've sat down, the toilet beside me flushes and I hear the unknown Woman unlock the door. I figure whoever else is in here must be fixing their makeup as I haven't heard the main door open or the sound of running water. All my nightmares come to life when I open my cubicle door to the face of my Stepmother. It takes a moment to register what she holds in her hand.... The letter from my Father.

"You took your time. I've been waiting in here for you since just after we arrived here. We need to have a little chat, don't you think?" Her face gives nothing away; every feature set in stone.

"A chat about what?" I try to ensure my 'gulp' is as inaudible as possible. She thrives off fear.

"Well, how is it fair that you get to live such a perfect little life when your Mother is the reason why my perfect life was ripped from me," I'm beginning to panic as somehow we've rotated so that she is nearest the door and I have no route for an easy escape.

"I didn't ask to be involved in this. No one asks to be born and no one can really choose the family they're born into. Why have you got my Dad's letter? Is that what this is about? You're jealous of my Dad's words to me?" My Stepmother laughs her wicked cackle and I slowly shrink into myself. That laugh never results in any-thing positive.

"You silly girl. Do you really think your Dad wrote this? I do have to say it was a treat to watch you read it. Your Dad wasn't proud of you, he hated you! You were forced on him because of your Mother's disgusting behaviour!" I'm shocked that she's taken things this far.

"That is so messed up. Forging a letter is just a new low, even for you! Is there anything else that you've masterminded?" I'm not sure I really want to know the answer to that question.

"Your Dad should've been more careful on those stairs," What. The. Fuck. What exactly is that supposed to mean. Her whole statement leaves so much to the imagination.

"What do you mean by that?"

She just smirks at me and tilts her head, giving nothing away as she nears me, ripping the note into little pieces as she does so.

Afterword

So here we are! The second book is complete! I still cannot quite put into words how amazing it feels to have a series out in the World.

I've always been one to doubt myself, but this has helped me to truly see that nothing is impossible.

Thank you to each and every one of my readers. The feedback I have received so far has been phenomenal and my life has a new meaning to it completely. So really, from the bottom of my heart, thank you.

This World has so much to offer. Go out there and be amazing.

Thank you again. Stay safe, well and happy!

- Susan x

Books By This Author

Watching Josie Martin

Life for Josie Martin is hard. Living with a Stepmother who hates her, and a Dad that pretends she does not exist, Josie can only dream of the day she finally finds true happiness again.

Nicholas (Nick) Peters likes the solitude of his private life. Save for his Uncle and best friend, Nick chooses to keep himself to himself.

Fate brings the two souls together and Josie is sure she has found her hero. Little does she know that there are skeletons in the closet; a life altering secret threatening to break through.

How long will Nick be able to keep the secret that threatens to crush the girl he has come to love?

Knowing Josie Martin

Josie's life has just taken an overly dramatic turn, one that she never saw coming. A big secret has come to light and Josie suddenly finds herself on a hunt for the full truth.

Nick finds himself in the middle of this catastrophe. The girl he has come to love is suddenly left heartbroken. Will he be able to piece together the fragments of Josie's broken soul, and will things ever be the same as they were?

About The Author

Susan Higgins

 Susan was born in Pembury, United Kingdom in 1998.

She began her writing journey at the age of 22 during the Covid-19 Pandemic.

Susan likes to associate her work to real World issues.

When she isn't writing, she likes to get out and admire the views around the Coastal Isle of Thanet where she resides.

Susan is due to begin University later on in 2021 to study towards a degree in Psychology.

For further updates from this Author, please take a look at the following Social Media pages:

Facebook: Susan Higgins Author

Instagram: @thisisshe_x

Webpage: https://www.susanhigginsauthor.com/

Printed in Great Britain
by Amazon

61649780R00081